Big Day,
Big Everything

☬ ✠ ☬

Anne O. S.

ISBN: 978-1-83709-266-6

COVER DESIGN BY: ART PAINTER
LIBRARY OF CONGRESS CONTROL NUMBER:
2018675309

Chapter One
Big Day, Big Dreams, Big Everything

People say Death can't be kidnapped. They're wrong. I know, because he was my father, and that was the day it happened.

That morning my hands shook, though I kept telling myself I wasn't afraid. It was supposed to be my big day, the one I'd waited for all my life. Dad's promise burned inside me. He would take me with him, show me everything, and teach me, since I was meant to follow as his successor.

I wanted it with such desperation that I counted the time. Two days. Three hours. All of them carved into my mind like scratches. 'For Deep's sake, I'll go mad if I count them once more,' I muttered.

Whether down or up, we were somewhere in between, in a kingdom called the Deep, though humans usually called it the Underworld or sometimes Hell.

My clothes were already waiting on the chair. It was a dark suit and a light blue shirt, both cut and stitched by Martus's cursed hands. He was my servant, though not by choice. My father had punished him years ago, turned his fingers into needles and his palms into thread, and from then on Martus had sewn without rest.

The punishment had started with me. I don't know... I was five, maybe younger, and, oh Deep, forgive me... I peed everywhere.

Martus hated it because Deepens didn't pee, and the whole idea disgusted him. He used to shout after me in despair: *'Tonny, not here! Not in the bathtub! Not on the floor... and for Deep's love, not on my plants!'* I'd laugh and do it anyway, because no one was allowed to scold me. My father saw it once, and instead of punishing me, he punished Martus, turning him into a tailor who would never stop sewing.

So that morning, when I buttoned the shirt and smoothed the sleeves, I tried not to think about any of that. I only thought about how the suit fit, how it looked, and whether I could pass for the man I was supposed to become.

Oh, for Deep's love... but I looked good. If elegance had a flavour, I'd be the kind of dish people never forget. Dark hair. Tanned skin. Tall. And the best part? Those green eyes were truly captivating. Deepers always said they stood out. I wasn't sure if that was true, but I liked the thought of it.

The nerves made it hard to breathe. After pacing the room once, then twice, I slipped my hand into my breast pocket. Hidden there was the small figurine I had stolen years earlier from a forgotten room in the palace. Ten centimetres of carved stone, no bigger than a child's toy, but it had been my secret companion ever since. Tapping with my fingertip, I whispered, 'Ready?'

Roddy, as I'd named him, didn't answer, but the silence comforted me all the same. A broad, white staircase of nearly two hundred steps waited at the end, each one gleaming like water that would not move. I placed my foot down, and the old mechanism stirred beneath me, carrying me smoothly downward, as if the palace itself wished to present me to the hall below.

My expectation was celebration: laughter, cousins waiting, tables of fruit and chocolate fountains because everyone knew how much I loved them.

I thought this would be the moment my life truly began. Instead, twenty servants stood in silence. Their heads were bowed, their hands folded, and not one of them met my eyes. Even before my feet touched the marble floor, I knew something was wrong.

It was as if the palace wanted me to feel each second of silence, and so the staircase dragged itself out slower than ever. By the time my shoes touched the marble, I was almost dizzy with the weight of it.

At first the words caught, scraping against the dryness in my throat, when I tried to ask where he was, until they finally broke out. The servant nearest me shifted as though he might answer, and for one moment I thought he would, but his mouth closed again, and the faint scrape of his boot against the floor was louder than anything he might have said.

So fast was my heart beating that I could barely hold my voice steady when I tried again, this time with more anger, to ask where my father was. No one spoke or lifted their head, and I knew without being told that something terrible and irreversible had happened.

And then Maria stepped forward, small against the marble pillars, her apron creased, her hands restless at her sides. The knot in my stomach came before her words, drawn by the sorrow in her eyes. Once she had been the one who scolded me, who brought me secret sweets and made the palace less cold, but now the warmth was gone.

'Tonny,' she said at last, 'your father hasn't returned.'

When the words landed, they spread through me like ripples from a stone falling into water. I wanted to get her to explain again, but my tongue felt too heavy, and the silence around us cut off the sound before I could shape it. Maria's eyes met mine briefly before lowering, and I knew she was telling the truth.

As if carved, the other servants kept their heads bent and hands folded. The hall seemed to close around me, and I felt smaller than ever before, because of their quiet and their stillness, and in that moment, I hated them for it.

Maria reached for my arm, her touch warm, and though I wanted to shake her off. I couldn't. My hand was trembling too much. She led me out, quiet on the marble, and I followed rather than drown in what I had heard.

The halls were dark, and even though I had run past those doors a hundred times, I had trouble seeing them. My thoughts circled too fast, colliding into one another; he couldn't be gone, he was Death, he always came back, he never failed, and still Maria kept her hand on my arm until we reached a wooden door at the end of the passage.

When she opened it, warmth came out. Unlike the palace halls, the kitchen felt lived in. It was smaller, warmer, with chairs that rocked unevenly and a table carved and stained by the years. Breathing in, the air tasted of sugar and woodsmoke; breathing out, I let it go slowly, as if the human world I had only read about in books might linger there a moment longer.

Maria poured a cup before I had even sat down. Sweet, thick vanilla cocoa, as she always made it for me. Waiting, she sat opposite after setting it in front of me, the small ladle that jutted from her collarbone clinking faintly against the table edge as she leaned forward.

Normally I would have drunk it with all the greed, licking the foam from my lips, but my hands only stirred the spoon in slow circles, watching the swirl collapse in on itself.

'Tonny,' she said gently, 'It's just... I don't know how to say it... he cannot die. You know that. So why are you so afraid?'

I stared into the cup as though the answer might appear in the ripples. My throat was tight, but my voice came out low, with a tremor in it.

'Because… It's the humans. They've taken him. I know it!'

Maria's lips pressed together, the way they always did when she wanted to argue but didn't want to hurt me. A strand of hair slid across her cheek, glinting with the thin wire threads that had grown there long ago. She reached for the pot and poured herself a cup, sipping carefully before setting it down again.

'Humans have tried before. They always fail.'

'Not this time,' I whispered. The spoon rattled against the edge of my cup as my hand shook, so I set it down quickly before she noticed. 'They must have found a way. I studied their world, remember? Their greed, their desperation. They never stop wanting what they cannot have.'

With a sigh, Maria reached across the table and laid her hand over mine, her palm cool and hard where the handle of a spoon had replaced two fingers. 'Tonny, you're half human yourself.'

'That doesn't mean I don't know what they're capable of. It means I know it too well.'

She didn't answer straight away. Instead, rising from her chair, she walked to the cupboard beneath the sink and bent down. As if debating with herself, she moved more slowly than usual, the small pan grown from her shoulder scraping faintly against the wood. When she straightened, a tin was pressed against her chest, hugged as though it were something precious.

I frowned. 'What is that?'

With a faint, guilty sort of smile, Maria carried it back to the table. From a teapot that seemed not to have seen the light in years, she poured after setting out two smaller cups.

The steam rose strong and bitter, carrying a scent I recognised at once.

'Maria,' I lowered my voice, even though no one else was there. 'That's tea.'

'Proper tea.' Her eyes glinted with mischief. 'Ah, Deep forgive me. English breakfast. From the human world.'

'It's banned!'

She waved a hand as if rules were nothing, the fork protruding from her elbow catching the light.

'Not everything from them is poison.' The cup slid towards me.

Carefully, I lifted it, staring at the dark liquid. The scent was sharper than cocoa, heavier somehow. Wet leaves and smoke tasted so strong that I almost coughed when I sipped. Maria drained hers in one long swallow, smacking her lips as though it were the finest thing she'd ever tasted.

'You see?' Already pouring herself another cup. 'Not all human things bring ruin.'

I tried another sip, slower this time, and let the heat settle in my throat. 'That doesn't change anything. They still have him. And if they've found it, if the whispers are true—'

Maria set her cup down, the smile fading. The wire in her hair trembled as though it, too, had heard. 'The stone.'

I nodded. 'Yes. The stone.'

The word hung between us, heavy as the silence in the hall had been. Neither of us spoke for a long while, the only sound the faint ticking of the old clock above the stove and the gentle scrape of my spoon against the cup.

I wanted her to tell me I was wrong, that it was impossible, that my father would walk through the door at any moment. But she didn't. She sat with me, holding the warm cup, and her eyes showed me the truth I denied.

Kitchen stillness became quite awful. Maria's cup was half-empty, mine still almost full, the steam curling away into nothing. I wanted to speak, but the words wouldn't form. And for a while it seemed easier just to sit there, stirring the spoon in circles, pretending the swirl might give me answers.

That was when the sound came.

At first it was distant, a low moan that seemed to roll through the stone itself, so deep it rattled in my chest. Maria stiffened in her chair, the pan on her shoulder knocking hard against the wood, her hand frozen halfway to her mouth. We looked at each other, wide-eyed, waiting for it to fade.

But it didn't fade. It grew.

The second time it came it was louder, so loud I clapped my hands over my ears, and still it poured through, vibrating in my bones. Maria gasped and dropped her cup, the tea spilling across the table in a dark rush. She staggered to her feet, gripping the chair for balance, the strange spoon-fingers of her hand clattering against the wood.

I had never heard that sound before, not once in my life, but the terror in Maria's eyes told me she had.

'Maria,' I shouted over the noise, 'what is it?'

Her lips moved, but I couldn't hear her. She crossed the kitchen, pulled the door open, and we both froze as footsteps thundered through the corridor. Servants were running, their faces pale, their hands fumbling with keys as they locked their doors behind them.

The sound finally began to die, leaving an emptiness even heavier than before. Maria turned back to me, her face drawn tight with fear.

'Tonny,' she said, her voice trembling, 'that was the Death Alarm.'

The name itself made my stomach twist. I had read about it in old books, the kind no one wanted me to see, but I never thought I would hear it myself.

Maria swallowed hard. The fork in her elbow twitched once before going still. 'Tony, it… it confirms it. Your father has been captured.'

The words landed harder than the sound itself, and for a moment I couldn't breathe. Captured? The word scraped through me like glass.

Maria sank back into her chair, her hands pressed to her face. One spoon-finger bent awkwardly against her cheek. 'And now… now they'll release the Dustdreads.'

The name shivered through me.

Dustdreads.

They weren't human, or angel, or demon. They weren't even Deepers. They were something else, something older, born of my father's own pain two hundred years ago when he had first been chained. I had studied them in secret, traced the fragments of stories others tried to forget. And every line I had read had chilled me.

'They'll come here?'

Maria lowered her hands. 'If we step outside, if we breathe their breath, we're lost. That alarm wasn't just for news. It was a warning.'

Pressing my palms against the table, I tried to keep myself steady. My father was gone. People had him. Also, Dustdreads would walk again. Deep help me. Help us.

Chapter Two
Cry of Souls

Dad's office was huge but not empty, filled with books, documents, parchments rolled onto bone holders, and maps of worlds I had never seen. But Dad knew them all by heart. A painting on the wall showed the soul crossing over. A glass case full of artefacts held strange objects that no one was allowed to use. A heavy table made of obsidian stood in the middle of the room. And in the middle of it all, there was me, Tonny. I was in a suit that was already starting to feel tight, with a little Roddy in my pocket that had started moving.

Stretching my ears, I found only quiet outside, the sort that weighs on you. In the Deep, it was never quiet. There was always someone shouting, dancing, cooking, arguing, or singing. But everyone was locked in.

Because of them. The Dustdreads.

A sigh slipped from me, quiet, as I looked out of the window. The courtyard was empty. One red leaf, left from the last Death Ornament, floated down and pressed against the glass.

'Is this not... weird?' I said out loud, even though I was on my own. Well... almost. Roddy shifted in my pocket. I felt it. 'You can talk,' I said slowly, like casting a spell.

Roddy coughed, gave a little buzz, and there was a soft click. A tiny chime sounded. From his flea-ridden body came a voice.

'It's not weird. It's dead.'

'That's a bit depressing, mate.'

'At least it's quiet for once. I don't mind it.'

'Oh, come on, things are serious in the Deep,' I said with a weak chuckle and pulled him out of my pocket.

I set him down on the table. He struggled to stay upright, since he was missing a leg, so he leaned to one side. Sometimes he toppled over completely. Faint runes flickered across his body. Some were totally unfamiliar. Some I remembered from Dad's books. One of them, right at the bottom, was my grandad's name. It was an old symbol that meant 'Death of the First Circle'.

'You know I was meant to see Mum today?' I said. 'It was our day. She wanted to take me to the Heaven Markets. Show me how it smells, how it looks, and what cloud sugar tastes like. Not that I'd be allowed to eat any.'

Roddy didn't say anything. His eyes blinked on and off, then on again.

'But how am I supposed to go if no one is allowed outside? And even if I could… how would I get through the gate? But… I have to go anyway. What if Mum knows something about Dad? Or someone up in Heaven? No, definitely not God, poor thing. But maybe in Hell? I know they searched for him there, yet still, something about all this doesn't sit right with me. Forget it — I won't get there anyway.'

Silence.

Roddy let out a rattling cough, like a cat with something stuck in its throat.

'You've got Martus.'

'So?'

'Get him to make you a coat.'

'A coat? You're going on about a coat now?'

'No. Not like that. A different one. I mean… you will look invisible. To them.'

'To the Dustdreads?'

'Yeah. They'll sense you like a whisper. Like a breath. They won't be sure if you're really there or not.'

'And he can actually do that?'

'That's the question, isn't it? Yeah. Especially if you've got me.'

I looked at him. He was small, old, and broken, yet there was something massive inside him.

'And what do you get out of it?' I asked.

'A trip. Finally. I want to see Heaven too. And maybe...'

'Maybe what?'

'Maybe there's an answer there. Alternatively, there might be a deeper explanation. Like you said... something stinks here!'

'Alright, Roddy. We'll find Martus!'

Bringing him up to my lips, I blew on him gently. If I overdid it, I knew he'd go off into some mad speech about crumbling worlds and kingdoms that don't exist.

He growled, blinked, and calmed down. A soft buzzing sound followed, like a sleeping cat. Quiet at last, he slipped back into my breast pocket as I gently slid him there.

'Have a rest, maestro,' I muttered, reaching for the door handle, ready to head out.

Click. I froze.

The sound had not come from the door in front of me. It had come from behind me, where it should not have come from at all. Slowly, as if I were scared of what I would see, I turned around. It had come from the side door. The forbidden one. The one that was always locked. Someone had just come out of it. The door shut quietly behind them. And out stepped a man.

It was Alan.

I recognised him straight away. He was tall and slim, wearing a dark green suit with black trim. Everything matched perfectly; even his round glasses and red beard glowed like freshly poured fire. But not in a cool way. More like… too neat. He was holding a thick notebook and had a map tucked under his arm. There was something in his eyes I couldn't read.

'Alan?'

He smiled.

'Tonny. I am sorry; I did not expect you would still be here.'

'Erm… it's alright. I just…' I nodded towards the door. 'What were you doing in there?'

I was not angry, just surprised. Really surprised. No one was allowed in there, not even me. It was not just some random room. It was a secret. Off-limits.

Alan stopped, adjusted his glasses, and said, 'Your father granted me access to that door some time ago. He gave me the key.'

The room went quiet.

Something fluttered sideways in my chest, like a fish trying to swim through glass. Dad? Gave him the key? And not me? I blinked. Something in me felt jealous, but I did not show it, of course. I just nodded.

'Right. Okay.'

Alan smiled again a little.

'I have been working on the inventory in there. Getting things ready in case something unexpected happens.'

'Like him disappearing?' I blurted out.

He blinked. Twice. I'm not sure if that was thinking or rebooting. Then the smile came back.

'For example.'

Silence came with him, and in passing he left behind the smell of old books and polished glass. I stood by the door a moment longer, then took a deep breath and stepped into the hallway.

Everywhere again, that same silence. I hated it.

Flames flickered without fire in the crystal alcoves that lined the corridor as I walked through. Anyway, we also had dancing lights here that never burned. They only lit up when someone walked past. I always liked that.

The walls were dark marble with thin golden veins that moved slowly, like they were breathing with the palace itself. Well... they actually were.

Underfoot, the floor shone with smooth obsidian, polished like a mirror. Our servants always had work to do here, and to be fair, they always did it well. Every time I caught my reflection in it, I looked taller than I really was and I loved it.

Up here, on the third floor, lived Deepers who had the most trust in the Deep. Overseers, masters, the ones who knew the rules… and sometimes the exceptions too.

Martus's room was right at the end of the west wing, by the Mirror Hall. No one usually came this way, so it was odd when I suddenly heard fast footsteps. The sound of shoes tapping on marble. The clink of a tray. A plate, and something gently rattling. A glass bottle?

Ducking into the shadows, I hid behind one of the arches that lined the corridor like a ribcage. From round the corner came an ordinary servant. A young Deeper, dressed in a silvery-grey tunic, carefully carrying a balanced tray. On it was a jug filled with dark liquid. Next to it sat a small glass bottle, bubbling blue, like a frozen storm was alive inside it. It fizzed, but quietly. The servant was heading straight for Maria's room.

I frowned and stepped out from behind the column.

'Err… you!'

The servant froze like a pulled wire. His head looked almost normal at first glance, but where hair should have been, thin straws stuck out in uneven bunches.

'M-M-Master T-Tonny?'

'What are you bringing to Maria?'

He blinked, unsure how much truth to tell. In the end he looked down, and as he did, sweat began dripping from the straws on his head, running straight into his mouth. He spluttered, unable to wipe it away, while I tried very hard not to look. Most of the time it was tea or juice trickling down those straws, but this was just disgusting, and I knew from now on I would never let him bring me a drink again.

'It's... j-j-just water and e-essence. She's not feeling well, apparently.'

'Not feeling well?' I repeated.

He leaned in closer and whispered.

'I heard... j-just a r-rumour, m-mind... that she drank a f-forbidden tea. And it m-made her ill. B-but we're not allowed to t-talk about it. N-no one is. If Death was here, h-he'd punish her.'

I was there. We drank that tea together. It burned my throat pretty badly, but of course, I didn't let on, I just nodded.

'Thanks. Take care of her.'

The servant bowed and quickly disappeared around the corner, his tray shaking in his hands, the straws on his head rattling faintly like dry reeds in the wind.

Forbidden tea… Oh Deep, poor Maria. I should not have let her drink it, but that did not matter now. I needed to see Martus.

I reached the door. These were different. Tall, dark wood, but smooth as silk. A fine needle-pattern carved into the centre looked like a moving web. Tiny pearls set into the wood glowed softly as I came closer.

Martus's door. I raised my hand to the knocker. It looked like an old seamstress with a long nose. And… I hesitated. I knocked, but nothing. Silence. I tried again, a bit harder this time.

'I am not opening,' came a voice from inside, gentle but brittle, like the voice of someone's grandfather telling stories by the fire.

I frowned. 'Martus, it's me.'

'That is exactly why I am not opening!'

I shook my head and placed my palm against the door. 'I need you.'

'You should have said that before you peed in my lavender, you little tyrant!'

I laughed. That was exactly how it had happened, but I knew he would let me in eventually. He just had to complain first, and sure enough, a few seconds later, the lock rattled. The door opened, and there he was.

Martus.

Massive, bearded, and stuffed into knee socks that had long lost their stretch. A plaster with a cactus drawn on it clung to one foot. He was small in height but thick in build, with a darker skin tone that made the glitter of his short white hair stand out even more.

'You look like you swallowed a rotten lemon and then rolled in moss,' I said.

'And you look like you were raised without supervision. Oh wait… you were!' he shot back, turning and walking in.

Deep wrinkles ran across his face, so many they almost glowed, and his ears were big enough to make him look half comic. And his hands? Not hands at all, but needle-like frames wrapped in loose threads that unwound and whispered with every move. He looked less like a man and more like some mad idea of a tailor crossed with a Christmas tree.

'Can I come in?' I asked.

'You are already inside. What do you expect me to do about it?'

I stepped inside.

Martus's room was not a normal bedroom. It was part workshop, part library, part forgotten greenhouse. His plants purportedly smelt like different emotions. Most had faded. Only in the corner, one bluish-green fern bush was still twitching, and it spat juice at me as I walked past.

'It likes you,' Martus said offhandedly.

'Almost as much as you do.'

'That sounds like an accusation.'

I sat on the stool next to his work table. A half-finished coat was spread across it. Threads moved in it like they were alive. Needles stitched on their own, slicing the air as if they were following some invisible pattern.

'I need a suit, or a coat,' I said.

'Fantastic. And I need hands!'

'Martus... please.'

'Oh, in heaven, hell, and the whole bloody Deep! That is a new one. Death's son knows how to say please? Is the end of the Deep closer than I thought?'

'I want a suit that'll protect me from the Dustdreads.'

He froze. His threads stopped all at once and stiffened with him. He looked at me. Long and quiet. Then he sighed.

'What are we talking about here? Invisibility cloak? Protective lining? Magical trousers?'

'Something that'll hide me. Like I'm not even there. Roddy said you'd know how.'

'That scrapheap still speaks? I should have thrown him in the pit with the rattling skulls years ago.'

'Martus...'

'No.'

'No?'

'No. I am not stitching you into anything again. And I am definitely not stitching you into death.'

'Then I'll die. And you'll be the one who let the last Tonny go.'

'Finally a bit of peace for me.'

We both went quiet. Then I looked up.

'I'll bring you the plant.'

'What?'

'The plant. The one that only grows once every hundred years. With bluish-purple leaves and a heart-shaped root.'

'You are making that up.'

'No. I know where it is.'

'It does not exist!'

'It does. In the fifth sealed chamber by the old elephant gate. Dad told me never to go there. So obviously I went all the time.'

Martus squinted at me.

'Bluish-purple heartleaf... I would plant that.'

'Exactly.'

'I would make tea out of it.'

'You can have a whole bath in it if you want.'

'Hmm.' He closed his eyes, muttered into his beard, then nodded. 'One piece. One job. But I am warning you. It will be stitched with all my bitterness.'

'You always did it that way.'

As I stood up, he grabbed my sleeve. The needles scratched lightly against my skin.

'Tonny… when your father comes back… beg him to give me my hands back.'

I stopped.

'Martus, of course. That'll be the first thing I do. I have asked him three times already.'

'Well… Maybe, you have not tried enough.'

'I'll try harder. Promise.'

Chapter Three
The Ivory Hall

Going into the forbidden parts of the palace was like saying to Deep, 'Go on then, eat me.' But honestly? I was used to it. This palace wasn't a house. It was a living organism. The corridors changed, stairs vanished, and the lights behaved according to the mood of the walls. In some parts, you couldn't breathe too deeply, or it would breathe you back in. And still, I knew where to go. I always knew.

'This is mad,' Roddy wheezed when I activated him in the corridor leading to the Ivory Hall.

'Yeah, I know.'

'The corridors are breathing. This place is hungry.'

'And you were meant to tell me where the plant is, not remind me it might eat me.'

'If you'd let me talk earlier, I would've told you between coffin scratches.'

'Which way?'

'Second on the right. Then straight. Then through shadow, not light. Light lies.'

I nodded and walked.

The Ivory Hall. That part of the palace was strange. It didn't quite fit in. All old wood, stone arches, forbidden boxes, and glass cases. Each item had its own energy, some humming faintly, others whispering at me.

Then I saw movement. Someone was there. A man, maybe. Tall, wearing a long coat, his face hidden under a hood or mask. He stood right between the shelves, just watching me.

In that moment, he vanished so fast it felt unreal, like he was never there at all. I took off after him, but...

'He is already gone,' Roddy hissed.

'You saw him too?'

'No,' he said, eyes narrowing. 'But I can feel it. Someone took something.'

I entered the hall. Everything was scattered. Boxes open, lids were torn, and some items from the cases were lying on the floor. One shelf was completely empty. A small box was missing. The lock was broken; the black seal split in half.

'What was in there?' I asked.

Roddy said nothing.

'Come on.'

'I don't know. I really don't. Oh look, over there,' Roddy suddenly pointed.

Behind one half-collapsed shelf, a plant was growing. Hidden, but glowing like a soul. Its leaves were bluish-purple, and the root... Oh yeah. Heart-shaped.

'I knew it exists!'

'Yeah, yeah, less chatting, more grabbing. Come on.'

I carefully pulled it out. Its stems let out a sigh, like they were saying goodbye. As I turned to leave, I caught something in the corner of my eye. Behind the shelf, under a cracked wooden display case, I spotted something small. I carefully picked it up. It was a porcelain doll.

Small, half-broken, but beautiful. Her arms were thin like tears, and her face was painted in a way that made her smile even after all these years. She had lace clothes that crumbled between my fingers. When I turned her over, she had a little key in her back, but I didn't wind it. Who knows how old she is or what she even does.

For a second, I completely forgot why I'd even come here.

'Roddy,' I whispered. 'Alright. We've got everything, now go on and sleep.'

He crackled, blinked, and then clicked softly shut. I put him in one pocket. The doll in the other. That one's for Amelia. She always loved broken things. Once, she found a cracked teacup in Hell's kitchens and said, 'It still holds warmth, that's enough.' On the way to Heaven to see Mum, I'd stop by her too. Because she loved old things, I knew she would like this doll. Especially the forbidden ones, the ones that didn't belong to her, and the weird ones.

Amelia was my fiancée. Well… fiancée. The thing is, we loved each other. Really loved each other. Only, Deepers weren't allowed to marry outside. It was an old law. Amelia was from Hell. Yes, daughter of Satan himself, and he wasn't exactly my biggest fan. He could not show it too openly, since, if I am honest, my dad was his king. Without him, Hell wouldn't exist, and really, neither would Heaven, but I'll figure it out. Once Dad comes back, I'll marry her. End of.

Mum couldn't be forgotten. I had to bring her something. Only now, with Maria sick from the tea we drank together, she wasn't going to bake any cakes. But that was alright. The heart-shaped chocolates she loved were the ones I took to her. Wrapped in gold paper, and when you unwrapped them, inside were two layers: bitter and sweet, just like life. Or me.

There. Flower in hand, doll close to my heart, plan in my head. And I was finally heading back to the door where Martus was waiting. I just hoped that invisible suit worked. Hoped it would not kill me. I would not even be surprised if Martus wanted revenge, but no. Martus would never. He loved me, and I loved him too.

I knocked. Twice. Then three times. Then once more, just because I was enjoying it.

'Come on, Martus,' I called. 'I've got what you wanted!'

There was some swearing from inside, something got knocked over, and then a quiet, 'Coming, you bringer of doom.'

The door opened with that classic dramatic creak of his, as if there was not a room behind it but another dimension. And there he was. Martus. In all his grumpy, knitted, needle-covered majesty.

'So where is it?'

'What do you mean?'

'Well, the plant. That heart-shaped bluish-purple one that does not exist. Except... you are holding it in your hand.'

I handed it to him. Carefully, like a child giving a parent something they stole from a museum. Martus took it and sniffed it. His eyes softened for a second... And then he coughed.

'Ugh. Smells like spoiled trust. Brilliant.'

Before I could say anything, he was already turning, muttering into his beard and disappearing into the workshop.

Among piles of fabric that moved on their own, I stood, facing one animated spool of thread that was very clearly swearing at me under its breath. A few minutes later, he came back.

'Done,' he said, wearing the grin of someone who knew he'd nailed it and wanted the room to notice.

'What? That fast?'

'I am a sewing machine, boy. Literally.'

And then he handed it to me. I stared at it for a moment. It was made of fabric. Black. Softly shiny. And...

'Are these... boxer shorts?'

'No. They are protective shorts with invisible thread, soaked in fear magic, which confuses Dustdreads and creates a shadow aura around your physical presence.'

'So... underwear.'

'Boxers. Do not insult me.'

I lifted them carefully between two fingers. They were... well, delicate. There was a little embroidery on the side — a skull, winking. Nice.

'Martus, you promised me a suit!'

'This is the base. Function test. If you survive, I shall stitch the rest. Socks included.'

I gasped. 'But how am I supposed to go across Deep in just underwear? I am Prince of the Deep!'

Martus's grin was criminal. 'Seeing you humiliated? Priceless.'

I clenched my jaw.

He sighed.

'Alright. I shall go pick you out a cloak as well, so you do not feel like you are in some bloody ski carnival. But you are wearing the boxers. They are magical.'

'Hm, thanks a lot, Martus.'

Martus disappeared into the back chamber, and I was left standing with magical boxer shorts in my hand, with which I was apparently supposed to save the world. Brilliant. I almost expected him to throw in a pair of socks with pom-poms.

Leaning against the table, I held the doll for Amelia in my other hand and ran through in my head how I was going to explain to the heavenly guards why I was trying to cross the gate in nothing but underwear with a porcelain toy.

Behind me, I could hear Martus mumbling. Probably cuddling the plant.

'My little photosynthetic miracle,' I heard him whisper. It was a soft whisper that sounded, well, actually kind.

But then the silence changed. It came from outside. At first, it was just a sound, like wind that had wandered into the wrong corridor. A sort of breath, only deeper and heavier. I scratched my wrist. Dust. The threads had stopped moving. One of them lay flat, as if it had fainted. Martus was still whispering to the plant, but his voice was lower now, as though he too could feel the weight pressing through the walls. I kept still, hardly daring even to blink. In the corner the light flickered once, not quickly, more like it had changed its mind.

Then a scream rose. It was not the sound of a Deeper, nor was it quite the cry of a beast. It was closer to the tearing of a soul that had not yet understood what was happening to it.

Martus froze and let the plant fall back into its pot. I looked up, and together we went to the window in the corner. It was long and narrow, dirty with age, yet the view from it was always wide, showing the courtyard and what lay beyond.

This time we saw the Dustdreads.

There were a hundred of them, maybe more. They were tall and heavy, with long black hair and thick black armour. Their faceless, dark shapes chilled the air around them.

In the middle stood one of our own, a Deeper who seemed to be a servant. He still held a tray in his hands, as if he had gone to fetch cakes and had lost his way. Now he stood trapped among them, blinking in confusion, as though he had walked into the wrong room and could not find the door.

Before I realised, I was at the door with my hand on it.

'No,' said Martus. His voice was quiet, his needles catching my shoulder. 'It is too late.'

'He's out there on his own,' I breathed.

'I know.'

'I can't leave him like that... I mean... they will...'

'I know... there's nothing we can do... nothing, Tonny.'

One of the Dustdreads stepped closer and paused. It did not touch him. It simply leaned in, slow, silent, and... sniffed. The servant froze, swallowed hard, and his eyes filled with tears that never fell. The whole tray shook with him. The look on his face was unforgettable. I wanted to scream, to run to him, yet I could not move or even open my mouth. I could do nothing but remain where I was, watching helplessly, as the servant slowly withdrew and was gone.

Where he had stood, only black dust floated through the air, and the tray lay on the ground. The Dustdread straightened up and walked away, as if nothing had happened.

Head spinning, fingers trembling, Martus held me tightly. His needles dug in a bit, and his coat smelled like burnt thread and wet stone, but I didn't mind.

'This cannot be undone,' he said.

Like a nightmare sure of its time, the monsters outside shifted like mist as I looked on.

Then the scream came again. But it was not a scream. It sounded like the cry of souls that had forgotten they used to belong to someone. There was rage in it. There was pain in it. And there was fear in it.

We stood there, still staring at the emptiness, where the servant had been.

Martus let go. Slowly.

'Are you sure you want to risk it? Your mother is alright, Tonny. You saw her last weekend,' he said.

'Well… you're right. I… I'll think it over,' I said.

'Don't be upset, Tonny. What is meant to happen will happen, and this… this is simply part of our lives,' said Martus, his head lowered.

'Really? You don't even believe that yourself. You're upset too, and now you're trying to tell me this is nothing?'

'I'm not saying it's nothing, I just…'

'Forget it,' I said, and walked out of his room.

Chapter Four
Invisible

On the bed in my room, I crouched over those stupid boxer shorts. Magical and protective, infused with invisibility, yet still only boxer shorts. I wondered when exactly my life had taken this turn.

For a moment, I hesitated before putting them on. They were surprisingly comfortable. Sort of soft and stretchy, and the moment I pulled them up, they disappeared. Well, not literally. But I did. For real. I looked in the mirror, and I was not there. There was neither a shade nor a reflection. Nothing but nothing.

'Well then... It actually works,' I muttered to myself, even though no one could hear it.

Then I picked up my trousers and tried pulling them on over the top, and in that instant, there was a click, like flicking on a light. Bam. And I was visible again.

'Brilliant,' I sighed. 'Martus knew what he was doing. Must be in the fabric. Or in the humility.'

Roddy woke up at that moment.

'See? Told you it works. Except... you've got to be naked, or Deep will betray you.'

'That sounds like your life motto.'

'Put it on a crest.'

Dark green, scuffed but solid, the rucksack waited. Into it I packed trousers, a shirt, shoes, and a light coat, a plan B for the other side of the gate. Roddy I wrapped in between the shirts, leaving him a little hole to breathe, or whatever it is he actually does.

'You're stuffing me in with your socks. Classy.'

'If you keep moaning, you'll end up next to the boxer shorts.'

'Death number five. Let's go die again.'

I had everything. I could feel it. My heart was beating a bit fast, but not from fear. That same kind of buzz you get right before you do something heroic. Or stupid. Or both. Usually both.

The rucksack lay open, and before closing it I carefully placed the doll inside. That little porcelain one for Amelia. I wrapped it in cloth so nothing would happen to her, and underneath it, I tucked a small box. Chocolates for Mum. The heart-shaped ones. Wrapped in gold paper that rustles like a memory. Like life and her, it was both bitter and sweet.

Roddy wriggled among the socks.

'Bit too many feelings here, Tonny. You're starting to sound like a love letter.'

'Someone's got to write it for me when I die.'

My heart was still racing as I closed the rucksack. Not from fear. Just that same strange kind of excitement that comes when you know you're about to jump.

Each step fell into quiet. No one heard a thing, since I was invisible. Only the rucksack on my back looked a bit like a floating green ghost, but Roddy had promised me the Dustdreads wouldn't notice. He said they were blind to emotions, or something like that.

In front of the palace, I stepped onto the courtyard and looked up at the sky. And... it hit me. I was actually going, not pretending, but heading out where it isn't safe.

In Deep, everything had its place and its door. But if you wanted to leave Deep, you couldn't just go up. We did it through the wall. Old, massive, and carved from a material that never gets rained on and never gets boring to look at. It had two gates: one to the left, leading to Hell, and one to the right, leading to Heaven.

The path to it was long. That was on purpose, so everyone could think it through before they made the biggest step of their life. And I was making that step. In boxer shorts.

All around me walked the Dustdreads. They were black figures. Tall, massive, with bodies covered in slime that shimmered even in the dim light. Each of them had a black, shapeless helmet, like someone had banned them from having a face. No eyes. No teeth. No mouth. And still the fear coming off them crept under your skin like thorns.

Heavy, slow clacks on the courtyard's stone tiles, each step like the world choosing its next to crush. Roddy was in the rucksack, completely silent. Really silent. Maybe even he knew that the fun had ended here.

'Don't be afraid, Tonny,' he whispered.

'Thanks for that. Saying it now while there's a storm in my boxer shorts,' I whispered back.

He was right. The Dustdreads didn't see with eyes. They sensed fear. And I... well, I was trying to be brave. I really was. And then I tripped. Caught my heel on my own boxer shorts, because of course I did, and before I knew it, I had lost my balance. I landed on my arse, the rucksack flew out of my hand, and at that exact moment, I became visible.

The boxers slipped down a bit. Not much, but just enough for the spell to stop. And in Deep's name, that one monster saw me. The silence around me stretched tight for a second, like a string pulled to its limit. Then one of them sensed me.

It slowly turned its head, or whatever was closest to being one, and began moving towards me. Step by step, like no one had ever told it that something so slow could be more terrifying than an explosion.

Right in front of me it stopped, then leaned in. Far too close. Its body shimmered as if it were coated in something living, slime that would never wash off. It stank in a way that cannot be compared to anything. Not like bad eggs. This was something else entirely, the kind of smell that happens when the body itself is afraid.

Then it started sniffing me. Not with a nose. It did not have one. But the front of it moved even closer, as if it were tasting me through the air.

I was trying to be brave. I truly was. But it was so close I could feel the fear coming off it, not just radiating, but being made fresh, like the creature created it with every breath.

'I'm... I'm Death's son...' I managed to get out.

The Dustdread pulled back slightly and made a sound that was neither a laugh nor a scream. Something in between, like when a storm laughs through the hollow of a dead tree. Then it whispered directly into my head.

'Liar. I smell human on you.'

It felt like a slap to the soul. He hit it exactly. Then he moved closer again. Even closer.

And I… could not take it anymore.

I threw up.

Yes. Just like a little boy. Into the grass, into the dust, right in front of that thing. And in that moment, something changed. The Dustdread froze, then turned towards what had come out of me. He knelt down and began to lick it. No, seriously. It was so disgusting I nearly threw up again.

The creature was literally snuggling what I had just vomited, as if it were the greatest delicacy in all of Deep. And me? I used it.

I got up, quickly but quietly. I left the rucksack. There was no time. I was back in the boxers. This time, they stayed on, and I ran. Across the courtyard I ran, slipping between black helmets that did not sense me. Maybe I had just stopped sensing myself. But I was alive, and for now, that was enough.

The wall was bigger than I remembered, or I was smaller inside. Cold like a thing and not like a friend, his body felt wrong, and though I held Roddy gently in my hand, he was completely off.

I looked over my shoulder. The Dustdread that had caught me was still kneeling, and now others were joining him. They stood around him like a cult of worshippers… of vomit. If it had not been so disgusting, maybe it would have been fascinating. But it was time to go.

The boxers shorts were still holding when I pulled them up. I was invisible. Good.

On the cold stone I placed my palm. The wall gave a low hum, like something that had finally woken up after centuries, and to the right, the gate slowly lit up. There was a thin line of golden light along the wall, and then the doors silently opened.

Entering, I paused for a little moment before exhaling. Inside there were Dustdreads too. They stood in the distance, not too close, but they were there. Given the fact that they did not see me, they were aware that something was wrong. I wasn't going to find out what they'd do if they came closer.

After that, I moved on in a quick and quiet manner till I stood at the Great Gate. It was huge and radiant, just like I remembered it. I had grown used to it by now, since I had passed through it a few times before when I went to visit Mum. She was always there, waiting just beyond the gate, smiling with her arms open.

Today? Nothing. The gate was shut, and the silence around it felt intense and strange.

In front of it stood Gateman. He looked like an angel at first glance, but in truth, he was more of a gatekeeper. He had no wings, not because he had lost them, but because he had never needed any. His hair was golden, his eyes were light, and the glow surrounding him was so strong that even Deep would have had to back away.

From the time I was little he had known me, and I had always liked him, but now it was not the same. I was invisible, and he simply could not see me, which turned out to be rather annoying, considering the situation.

'Er… Gateman?' I whispered.

Nothing.

'Hello?'

He scratched his head and looked around, scanning the air.

'This isn't funny,' he muttered to himself.

I smiled because I simply could not resist it, and I gave him a little pinch on the arm.

'Ow!'

He turned quickly, looking around like a startled deer.

'What was that?!'

I bent down, picked up a small rock from the ground, and tossed it at his foot.

'OW!'

Now he looked genuinely alarmed.

'What is this? A ghost? A demon? The Guardian of the Gate does not get scared! I have a protocol!'

'Calm down, it's me,' I hissed.

'Who's me?!' he shouted.

'It's me. Prince of the Deep. Remember?'

Silence.

'Tonny?' He narrowed his eyes. 'Where are you?'

'Right here. In front of you. I'm just... sort of... well...'

'What?'

'In my boxer shorts.'

There was a short pause. The surrounding glow dimmed just slightly.

'Wait... you're naked?'

'Not exactly. I'm wearing magic boxer shorts. Martus made them for me.'

'Martus... the one with all the needles?'

'Yes, that one. And they work. I'm invisible.'

'Then why did you pinch me?!'

'I wanted to check if you were still the same.'

He shook his head.

'You really haven't changed.'

At last, he raised his hand, placed it against the golden stripe running along the gate, and it slowly began to open with a deep, smooth sound, like stone sliding over stone.

'Come in, Oh Invisible One in the Trousers,' he said in a serious voice.

'I'm getting that engraved on a plaque,' I replied.

'Let's hope nobody else spots you. Your dignity wouldn't survive even a minute.'

'My dignity died somewhere between vomiting and running away without my rucksack.'

Chapter Five
Just One Little Bird

Through the gate I stepped, onto a path of white gravel, walking quietly without leaving shadow or footprint behind. There was no rucksack either. That had stayed behind in the Deep, along with the last bits of my dignity. The boxer shorts were still holding, thanks to Martus, but I wasn't sure how much longer I could go on like this. It was warm, and walking around Heaven half-naked, even though no one could see me, had its limits. It was especially difficult in a psychological sense.

Heaven felt peaceful. Maybe a bit too peaceful. Everything smelled like vanilla, the flowers looked perfect, and the paths were smooth and spotless. There was no dirt, no pain, and no screaming.

Then I heard a voice.

'God, please… just one little bird, yeah? A tiny one that sings. Maybe sits on my shoulder. That's not too much, is it?'

I stopped. Standing on the path was one of them. Blond hair, wearing a tunic, with that same calm smile everyone had here. And then it happened.

Plop.

A bird dropping landed right on his forehead. He stood still, slowly reached up to touch it, blinked, and said in the most peaceful tone possible, 'Oh no. God's having another Monday.'

I chuckled. There was no stopping it.

'Hello?' he called. 'Is someone there?'

'Unlucky, mate,' I whispered.

He froze.

'Who...?'

'I'm here. It's me... Tonny. I am just invisible.'

'Invisible? Why?'

'Magic boxer shorts. Long story, trust me,' I said.

'Oh. That actually sounds fair enough.'

I smiled. We walked side by side for a bit, me unseen, him with bird poo on his face.

'Hey... you haven't seen my mum today, have you?' I asked.

He thought about it.

'No. But she's probably at home. She usually is.'

I nodded. That did sound like her.

'Aren't you worried, being out like this? You do know... the Dustdreads...'

He laughed softly.

'There's no fear in Heaven. It just doesn't exist here.'

'Take care,' I muttered as I turned down a narrow lane leading to Mum's house.

I was close now. I could feel it.

Everyone here looked the same. They had this strange glow to their hair, and their faces were smooth and untouched, like time had skipped over them. Not a wrinkle, not a single line. None of them remembered who they used to be. It gave them peace to forget, yet for me the burden was heavier. I remembered, and being the only one who did left me in a cold, lonely place.

There weren't many souls here. It was quiet and small. Everyone knew each other, even if they weren't friends, they were familiar. Rare were the good souls; Hell, however, was crowded, overflowing, endless in its growth.

At last I came to the door. The house was white and small, its stillness almost fragile. Curtains hung gently in the windows, and roses opened beneath them, just like I remembered.

I didn't knock. There was no need.

Here, if you stood at someone's door, they already knew. The moment you arrived, they felt it — saw it, maybe, in that strange way souls do up here. Like a thought whispered straight into the heart.

So I just stood there, knowing she knew I was on the other side. And still, I couldn't bring myself to go in. In Heaven no one remembered a thing. My mum was different: she remembered everything, since death had never come for her.

When I was born, my father literally pulled her out of the world of the living. Not as Death, but as a man who couldn't bear to lose the one person he loved differently from all the others. Only, their love wasn't a fairy tale. My father loved her in his own way. And she… well, she mostly endured him.

The Deep was somewhere she never wished to live. It frightened her, maybe because of my father, maybe the darkness, maybe the rules. Her place was Heaven. She was the only living woman among the dead.

When I was a kid, I used to come here on weekends. Dad worked too much. And I… well, I was just a child. They passed me back and forth like a book without a bookmark, but Mum cared about me. In her own way.

She was strict, no doubt about it, but even though she didn't smile often, when she did, it felt like the world finally made sense.

I still remember one of those moments.

Dad dropped me off here once when I was about six. I sat on the front steps, licking a lollipop, one of those he used to bring back from the human world, and listening to them argue inside.

'I had him on Wednesday,' Mum said firmly.

'What? Are we doing this again? Fine, I'll leave him at the palace,' Dad grumbled.

'Leave him if you want, but make sure he's got a full belly, understood?'

And then she smiled and took me in anyway. Just like always.

She always had her famous heavenly biscuits ready for me. I loved them. They were round, soft, and smelled of lemon and honey, and she swore they were filled with joy. To me, they mostly tasted like sugar and butter, but I loved them all the same.

The door opened slowly with a quiet little click.

Mum stood in the doorway. There was no one in front of her. Just air. She looked around once, then again, and then let out a soft sigh.

'Oh God… I need something for Tonny to wear.'

From the sky, something rustled and drifted gently down to the doorstep. It was a T-shirt with glittery letters that read 'Dangerously Angelic', and a pair of trousers one size too big, with one belt loop missing.

Mum looked down at it and raised an eyebrow slightly.

'Yeah. Classic.'

The door stood slightly open behind her after she turned her back. I stood there, invisible, just a few steps away, still in my underwear and absurdly grateful that Heaven had finally thrown me a bone.

Instead of stopping in the hall, I slipped quietly inside and went straight behind the curtain to dress, making not a sound. It wasn't much, just a few pieces of fabric, but the moment I pulled them on, I became visible again.

Inside it smelled just like it used to: clean, slightly sweet, and a little like someone who hadn't needed anything new in a very long time.

Mum was in the kitchen, quietly rearranging something in her jars, and without turning around, she said, 'So, where's your backpack?'

'Rucksack, mom and I left it with the Dustdreads. Long story, lots of slime.'

'Hm.' Instead of keeping it for herself, she sat at the table and offered me the biscuit. 'They're not fresh, but they're here.'

I smiled and took one. They tasted just like always, or at least that's what I wanted to believe.

'Dad is gone,' I said.

'I know.'

'There's panic in Deep. No one has any idea where he is. He didn't come back from the human world.'

'And you thought he would come back?'

Her reply left me speechless and frozen.

'What do you mean by that?'

'Your father likes to disappear. He rarely lets himself be found.'

There was a moment of silence, and then she added in a quieter, softer voice.

'But he's strong. If anyone can be lost and survive it, it's him. And you… you're just as stubborn as he is.'

I smiled, because that was probably the closest I'd ever got to hearing the words 'I love you'.

Then it hit me.

'The chocolates! Oh no, I…'

'That doesn't matter,' she said calmly. 'I don't eat sweets anyway.'

For a moment something stung in my chest. She'd always said she loved them. And I'd nearly had my face bitten off for them. But I stayed quiet.

After a while, she got up and walked to the window.

'You should go.'

'What?' I asked.

'Tonny… it's not safe here… I mean, not for you. Deep needs you. That's where you belong. Here you're just a visitor.'

I nodded, even though I didn't want to.

'And… what about Dad? I am worried.'

'He will come back,' she said without hesitation, then, after a brief pause, added, 'when he wants to.' She smiled at me and stroked my cheek. 'Go.'

Nodding, I stepped back toward the door and paused with my hand on the frame. Behind me, I heard her move.

From under the table she pulled out a small black box tied with an old blue ribbon, after pausing at the window and crossing the room.

She held it tight in her hands, and I heard her whisper, just barely, 'Hope you still make it, love.'

When she opened it, I saw the faint glint of photographs inside. Family pictures, ones she had never shown me but often looked at when she thought no one noticed. Her head bent low over them, her eyes shadowed and sad. I just left.

Chapter Six
The Blue Car

Not at the gate itself, but on a stone set slightly apart, I sat quietly. Being invisible once more, I watched the world turn as a strange quietness settled inside me. Mum was... different. Not that she was mean. Just... I don't know. I was expecting something else. More warmth. Something like 'come here' or at least 'just be careful'. Anything that would sound a bit like a mum. Instead, I got a biscuit and the sentence 'Go.'

Roddy shifted slightly in my pocket, so I took him out, blew on him, and he lit up.

'So how was it?' he asked.

'Fine,' I answered without thinking.

'Uh-huh. Fine as in 'I went there and no one wanted me', or fine as in 'my mum loves me, she just doesn't know how to say it'?'

I frowned.

'Look, she just... wasn't in the mood, yeah? Maybe it's all too much for her. Dad, Deep, the world... all of it at once.'

Roddy was quiet for a moment. Then he said, in a completely calm voice, 'she never really wanted you, you know that?'

I froze.

'That's not true,' I said slowly.

'But it is. I can see it on you. You were trying to dig out even a bit of love from her. And you know what? You just kind of... made it up.'

'Shut up,' I said quietly, without anger.

'Sorry. But I only lie to you when you overheat my system.'

We were still sitting together. Above my head, little birds were flying around that looked like bubbles, and under my feet were thoughts that didn't belong to me.

I was sad. Sad about Dad. About someone who at least understood me a little, because without him the world felt quiet and directionless, like someone had switched off your inner compass.

'Hey, don't you want to go to Hell?' Roddy asked.

'Excuse me?' I raised an eyebrow.

'Maybe they know something there that we don't. And...'

'And?'

'And you've got that Amelia of yours, right?'

A smile spread across my face.

'Well... that's actually not such a bad idea.'

Hell. It's just around the corner. Well... down through the gate on the left, knock three times, kick once, don't trip over a skull.

And I was invisible still, boxer shorts on, Roddy in hand. Right in front of the gate to Hell I was standing. Black wall, golden frames, doors with ornaments that looked like they were breathing.

And just ahead of me, only a few metres away, stood her. A tall figure in a red tunic, hair like coals, eyes glowing like molten gold. Hellish elegance in its purest form. And a face that tells you she's got time for everything but could eat yours any second.

I took a deep breath.

'Hello, Gateman,' I said.

And there was a long silence. Heavy, unsettling silence.

'What did you just say?'

'Um... Hello?'

'No. You called me Gateman. I am Gatewoman.'

'Look, I'm sorry. I'm just nervous... and in shorts.'

'I know. Your tricks don't work on me. Prince of Deep.'

She raised her hand, snapped her fingers, and something clicked. Everything went dark. Not literally, but something shifted.

'Wait… what did you do?'

'A little hole.'

'Where?'

'Guess.'

Exactly at that moment, I felt a pleasant breeze. In a place where there absolutely should not have been any breeze.

'You're joking!' I shouted.

'Hell's rules. And my nerves.'

'So what, half my arse is showing?!'

'No. Just a third. I'm not a monster.'

At last, she stretched out her hand and sliced the air open. She created a passage. Light. Heat. Hell. 'Go. And don't get lost. If you do, at least you'll stop calling me Gateman.'

I just shook my head I stepped in. With a hole in my dignity. Excellent.

Behind the Gate, it was quiet. Suspiciously quiet. Hell usually vibrates with laughter, music, shouts of joy and cheek. But today? Nothing. Curfew applied here too.

I stood on the edge of red paving. There was a breeze. And I was only ninety percent invisible. Roddy trembled ominously in my hand.

'Why… why me, Tonny?' he said quietly.

'Don't be a drama queen. I'm covering you with my body, not my soul.'

'This is abuse of an ancient artefact. I want a solicitor.'

'This is Hell, Roddy. Solicitors are retired here.'

I was trying to cover my arse using my hands, Roddy, and the last bit of dignity no one had taken seriously in a long time. By the way, I had loads of cousins here, and quite a few mates too. Of course, they weren't human. And they weren't demons either, as the world tended to think.

It was a bit different in here. Not different in a dramatic way, just gently shifted, strangely bent, but still beautiful in its own way. I loved it here. At least it wasn't as boring as Heaven. There were no children here. None at all. That was because children were purely a human thing. My cousins came from royal blood. They were born as babies, yes, but the moment they arrived, they were already grown. They came with eyes full of centuries, chests like stone, and a sense of humour that never got old.

Not all of them were made like Deepers. Some were created in completely different ways, and others simply came into being without explanation. Dad's brother lived here as well. He was my uncle, and he really liked me.

He was a good man. He didn't put on airs, not even about power, even though he could easily have claimed it. He had that strange kind of calm you wouldn't find in Deep or in Heaven. But his son was a different story. He was one little mistake that simply shouldn't have happened. Born right, he carried a body straight out of an anatomy book, two metres in height with shoulders like doors. But the brain? That stayed childlike. It just stopped somewhere along the way and never moved on.

So my uncle looked after him. He spoiled him, let him play with toys, puzzles, and little cars. Most of them were blue, because Gabriel loved blue best. And that was where I was going now. I was heading to them. To their manor, which smelled of oil, plastic, and biscuits.

There was no way I would visit Hell and not visit my family. That would be the end of all worlds. And perhaps I would find an answer there. Maybe I would get a hug and, if nothing else, I was hoping for at least a proper pair of trousers.

My uncle's house looked, how else, properly hellish in style. It was carved from black stone on the outside, but the windows had curtains with little ducks. There was a red carpet at the front door. Really. But no one cleaned it, so it was covered in soot and looked more like an ashtray than a fancy welcome mat.

I knocked, probably with an invisible hand, while holding my arse with Roddy and my elbow, because the boxer shorts hissed with every move and the draught was crawling right up the back of my soul.

The door burst open, and there stood Gabriel.

A two-metre giant with red, messy long hair, a unicorn T-shirt, and the expression of a kid who had just decided that today was absolutely brilliant.

He smiled, raised his hand, pointed right at me, and shouted with delight as if he had just won the lottery, 'YOOOOOU! YOUR BUM'S OUT!'

Jumping up and down, he made the whole house shake. Body like a mountain, but pure childlike joy on his face. But I loved him. He was cute.

'Gabriel…' I started gently, switching to that tone you use with toddlers or very nervous small dogs. 'Where's Daddy, hmm? And why are you here alone? You know you're not supposed to open the door, don't you?'

Gabriel stopped, blinked, and then stomped so hard the skeleton bear on the garden swing snapped loose.

'I WANT A CAAAAAAARRRRRRRRR!'

And launched into a tantrum. An epic one. He threw himself to the ground, arms flung into the air, legs kicking like propellers. No tears, but the sound? Like a full-on demon exorcism. 'I DON'T HAVE A BLUE CAAAAARRRR! NOBODY GAVE ME ONE! EVERYONE'S MEAN!'

'Gabriel, sweetheart, calm down,' I tried to keep both dignity and authority. 'Uncle Tonny hasn't got a car, but I'm sure we'll find one together. How about that?'

'NOOOOOOOOOOOOO!' he yelled and started rolling down the hallway like an out-of-control meteor.

By then, the servants had finally arrived.

One of them was carrying a tray, the second a pillow, the third a doll that looked like a mini-Satan, and the fourth was holding a blue plastic suitcase that was making a sort of buzzing noise.

'Master Gabriel is having an episode! Careful! Don't touch him directly!'

'Play him a song! Quickly! Where's the magic gramophone?!'

'Tonny? Are you alright?' one of them asked, then paused. 'Erm... erm... you've got... a draft.'

'Yeah. Long story,' I said.

Meanwhile, Gabriel was lying on his side, smacking the ground with his hands and shouting something about betrayal and blue hell. The servants had started gently wrapping him in a blanket and stroking his head like they were calming down a giant hot-air pancake.

'We'll get him the little car from the bedroom, yes?' one of them whispered.

'Do it, or he'll bring the whole floor down.'

'Tonny… you're brave.'

'I've got a hole. So we're even.'

At that moment, there was a heavy footstep from the stairs, followed by a voice that managed to drown out even Gabriel's dramatic 'NOOOOOO!'

The thudding rolled down like an avalanche, along with a rush of air that felt like a barrel tumbling down the steps.

Uncle.

He was short and round, bald, with darker untouched skin, wearing a dressing gown embroidered in gold with the words *HELL IS HOME*. Looking like a man happy to make pancakes in a nuclear bunker, he smiled, and the plaster cracked.

'Tonny, you lost mug! If you'd let me know you were coming, I wouldn't have sent Gabriel to the door. And now we've got a disaster on our hands.'

Gabriel lifted his head from under the blanket and shouted with joy:

'DAAAD, I'VE GOT A CAAAAAAR!' and in a burst of excitement ran straight into a pillar.

Uncle didn't even blink.

'Come on in, lad, come in,' he said, tilting his head. 'You look... somewhat breezy.'

'Long story,' I muttered.

'Hell is a long story,' he grinned.

Soon I had clean, elegant clothes on. They were black, warmed by heat. Gabriel got a new blue car and was driving it round the table like he was piloting a tank with an exhaust pipe.

Uncle sat me down by the fireplace.

Yes, a fireplace. Because apparently, in Hell, there's no such thing as 'enough'. He sat across from me and handed me a glass of red liquid that smelled of cinnamon and smoke.

'Tonny... I was originally planning to visit you in Deep.'

'Why?' I raised an eyebrow.

'Because the Council is being called. The whole Council. God. Satan. All the leaders of the worlds.'

I froze.

'Because of Dad?'

'Because of something... more serious.'

He fell silent just as Gabriel did three skids across the carpet and shouted gleefully:

'BOOOOM!'

'People... aren't dying anymore.'

'What?!' I sat upright in the chair.

'Death in the human world has disappeared. So no one is leaving. And you know what happens when death stops. Earth overflows. And when it overflows... it tears. And with it, everything else.'

Silence. Only the flames in the fireplace kept whispering.

'Is this the end?' I muttered.

'No. But it's a threshold. And if we don't cross it properly... everything burns.'

He stood up and pulled something from his pocket. From a fold of cloth, he revealed a necklace: a black cord with a white stone that almost whispered cold.

'Wear this. The Dustdreads won't perceive you. They won't detect you. They won't feel you. But be warned: if you lose it... you're prey again.'

'I won't,' I nodded and put it on, and for the first time in a long while, I felt a sense of safety. Finally.

'So the shorts are going into eternal damnation?' I asked with a smile.

'If possible, immediately.' Then he pulled out a black envelope. It was heavy, kind of quiet, and sealed with power. 'Without this invitation, they won't let you into the meeting. Keep it on you. And return to Deep. A carriage is waiting. You have... two hours.'

'I understand.'

His eyes narrowed.

'Where are you headed now?'

'To... Satan. Just a quick stop.'

He blinked. Slowly.

'Alright. But don't take too long. And Tonny... be careful. Today no one can be sure who's watching whom.'

I nodded and stood up. The necklace was around my neck. The envelope was in my pocket, and then Gabriel grabbed my hand.

'Tonny?'

'Yes?'

'When you come back... will you bring me a red car?'

'Red? That's new! I swear on our worlds, I'll bring you the brightest red!'

'BLUE! I WANT BLUE!'

'Blue it is.'

Chapter Seven

Game

Outside in Hell, right in front of my uncle's place, I took a deep breath. Oh, hell and Deep's belly. I loved it.

That fiery, smoky, weirdly spicy Hell air? Yeah, it did something to me. Made me feel lighter. Relaxed. And, weirdly, always made me hungry. No idea why. Like the second I took it in, my stomach would start yelling about how unfair it was not to be full of something delicious.

Lucky for me, I was heading to Amelia's. She lived around the corner. Yes, in Satan's actual palace. Her golden father, the one I wasn't exactly besties with. He wasn't as bad as God, though. God was old. Like ancient carpet stains and bird poop kind of old. Honestly, Heaven needed an update. It smelled like expired promises and disinfectant. Satan was... different. Arrogant as anything. Walked around like the universe owed him rent. But his palace? That place had food. And I needed food.

I walked slowly, mostly because everything was dead quiet. The Dustdreads were out, which meant no souls wandering, no demons loitering, and thanks to my uncle I wasn't still walking around in my boxer shorts. That necklace he gave me? Total lifesaver. Literally.

Still, the quiet bothered me. You're supposed to hear the souls, even from behind the wall. Always wailing, always moaning. It was usually like a never-ending symphony of shame, but that day there was nothing.

It was weird.

And now I was standing in front of Satan's palace. To be exact, Amelia's. The same scary, huge doors. There was still time for me to get in. Prince of the Deep and all that. Doors had to respect the title.

Inside, the smell hit me first. Satan's teeth, down in the Deep, it was good. Like someone slow-roasted a dream. Meat, spice, warmth, a bit of smoke, and this sweet undertone that made you think of memories you were not even sure were yours. It was like tasting nostalgia in the air. I grinned without meaning to. This was more like it.

People always imagined Hell as nothing but chains and screaming, and sure, there was a department for that, but this palace? It breathed. Black marble stretched beneath my feet, obsidian shot through with gold veins that pulsed like dying embers. Rising around me, the red crystal pillars were tall and sharp as spears. When my sleeve brushed one, a cold sting bit into my arm. I jerked back. Yes. Death wish confirmed.

At first the walls looked smooth, but if you stared too long they shifted, as though something pressed from the other side. Shapes flickered there, faces perhaps, eyes widening, mouths stretched in silent screams. I blinked and they were gone. That was new. The walls had never moved before. They had never watched me. So why now?

Then came the sound. The chandeliers above, bone and chain dressed in silver, began to sway. The grinding turned into whispers. Faint at first, like dust sighing. Then sharper. Words.

'Death is gone,' they hissed. 'Hell will claim you.'

In the colder air my grin slipped away, and I tilted my head back slowly, denying them the sight of a flinch. Silver light dripped over me like cobwebs.

This had never happened. The chandeliers had never spoken. Hell had its tricks, but this? This was personal.

My hand twitched towards my blade, though I knew it would not help.

'Go on then,' I muttered.

Rattling harder, the chains knocked bone against bone like teeth, shadows sliding free of the walls to crawl across the floor. One crept over my boot, cold as grave soil, and I kicked it off, stepping back with my heart pounding.

The palace laughed, and the marble, the crystals, and the air shook. Hell had thrown plenty of fear at me before, but this was different. This one was a dare.

And then, 'Well, well. Look who finally turned up,' said a voice ahead.

Spinning fast and ready, I found him there: Figgy at the top of the stairs, smug as though he had been waiting for the show. Tall, too pretty for his own good, light hair in that perfect little ponytail, stupidly perfect coat in some shade of green I couldn't name but hated how good it looked.

'Didn't think I'd see you here,' he said, smoothing his hair with a flick like he was being filmed. 'Nice to see you too.'

'I'm just here to see Amelia.'

Crossing his arms, he said, 'I figured. You know there's a curfew, right?'

'Yeah, yeah. Got it under control.'

'Figgy, seriously, I don't have time.'

'Oh come on. Since you've been with Amelia, you've totally forgotten about us.'

'I have not. You know what, fine. One. Just one.'

He grinned. 'That's my prince.'

And off we went.

We passed through a hall I'd always loved. Black marble walls that pulsed gently, breathing in slow waves. Paintings whispered as we passed, murmuring names I didn't want to remember.

A few steps later, we were in the cellar. Just like that. We came into the room. It was that old, deep one full of shadows, the one I loved, and in the middle of it stood the Game Stone.

'Remember?' Figgi smiled.

'Last time you lost. Three times.'

'Three times because of you, because you kept distracting me with your speeches about how your teacher told you, you were special.'

Figgi smiled again, this time with pride creeping into his voice too.

'It wasn't just talk, Tonny.'

'Alright then, we'll see today who's special,' I replied and laughed.

Then he reached into his pocket.

'Today we're playing... a new version.'

The Game Stone shimmered like black glass with fine red cracks. The ceiling of the cellar reflected on its surface, along with Figgi's eyes.

He sat opposite me, completely calm. His fingers were steepled, his nails long and clean, and on one hand he wore a ring with an old crest I didn't recognise.

Next to the stone lay our markers. His were small crystals, elegantly cut and gleaming, while mine looked rough, almost like they'd been ripped out of a wall.

Figgi smirked when he looked at them.

'Deep taste, I assume?'

'Exactly, it's not about appearance. It's about weight.'

'Interesting approach,' he said, then stroked the board's surface and added,

'You know this version of Sutraka is one of the lost ones?'

'Doesn't surprise me. You've always had a thing for forbidden stuff.'

'This isn't about points, Tonny. We're playing for knots of reality. For soul, for influence, for who can reshape the very structure of the world.'

He took one of the crystals and flipped it through his fingers.

'Each of us has seven markers. Each move means pain… or power.'

'And what if someone loses?' I asked quietly.

'Then they forget. Maybe the name of someone they love, maybe even why they came here.'

The board was shaped like a seven-pointed star, and each point — each knot of reality — had its own power:

• Anger brings confusion into the opponent's move.

• Pain forces the opponent to sacrifice a marker.

• Fear blocks the opponent's move.

• Silence makes your own marker invisible.

• Memory restores a lost move.

• Fire doubles the knot's effect.

• Bond links two markers and creates a shadow move.

We started.

The first move was mine. I placed a marker on Anger and the board creaked, or maybe I did, because on the other side of the knot, the glass started to crack faintly.

Figgi reached for one of his crystals and smoothly placed it opposite me, on Pain.

'So, war,' I noted.

'It's a game, Tonny.'

'Yeah, but games tend to be more serious than reality.'

He laughed, and in that silence between inhale and exhale, I felt it. A wave. Soft, but definitely there. Figgi was cheating, not much at all, only a small twist in the knot, a bend in reality so tiny it was almost invisible.

I looked at him from the corner of my eye, but he was smiling and looking elsewhere.

'So… how's Amelia?'

With my hand on another marker, I said it casually.

Figgi hesitated for a moment; he had never paused before, not even slightly.

'She's fine,' he said quickly. Perhaps a bit too quickly.

'She does what she's meant to. As always.'

'You don't see each other much, do you?'

'I'm loyal to her father. That's enough.'

I slowly placed the stone on Silence. The whole board turned cold under my hands.

'Yeah, but you two see each other quite often, don't you? You always got along.'

Figgi smiled. But something flickered in his eyes. Something sharper. Something possessive.

'Of course. We grew up together. Like brother and sister. Almost.'

'Almost?'

'Well… sometimes the line between love and admiration is very thin,' he said with a laugh.

That wasn't an answer, but I let it pass.

The game continued, and he cheated again. Barely. Almost unnoticeably. He shifted the strength of the knot, redirected the flow of magic. I only placed my stones where he didn't want them.

And then, in a single move, I controlled three knots: Anger, Pain, and Fear. The board flickered briefly. Figgi froze.

'That's not possible…'

'It is. And it's also a rule. Remember?'

'The Ritual of Reshaping…' he murmured quietly.

I placed the final stone. The fourth knot. The board cracked. Only on the surface, like shattered glass beneath the feet of someone who had survived.

'The game is over,' I said.

Figgi remained seated, silent, expressionless. Then he stood.

'You're going to see her?'

'See who?'

'Amelia.'

'Yeah. I just wanted to tell her something. Say a few words.'

'Of course. Words…' He blinked slowly.

'Good luck, Tonny. Not everyone has what you do.'

'Well... not everyone is born a prince.'

'Right.'

Turning, I felt his gaze on my back, stripped of pain or envy, filled only with hunger. I left the cellar and returned to the corridor where the soft red glow still burned. Above me, that was where she might be waiting. The girl demons lie for, and heroes gamble their minds just to be near.

Amelia.

Anyway, Figgi: my old friend, who by now was sixty years older, give or take, but never stopped trying to keep up. Too polite. Too clever. And far too quiet when Amelia laughed. He never said it out loud. He didn't need to. I saw the way he looked at her when he thought I wasn't watching.

But she chose me. Of course she did. I'm Tonny. Son of Death. Eyes like fire, voice like a sealed promise. Figgi? He couldn't even win a game without cheating, let alone steal a princess's heart. He never stood a chance, or at least that's what I kept telling myself.

Sometimes three times a night.

The palace corridors wound like snakes. Walls murmuring names. The floor beneath my feet warmed me right through to the bone, even though I still had shoes on. Finally I was standing at her door.

I knocked. Twice.

The door opened by itself, slow as a theatre curtain, and there she stood. My Amelia. My amour. Wearing a gold-red dress with a high collar and sculpted shoulders, she carried golden curls, green eyes, and lips bright with dangerous red. If her darker skin caught the light and sparkled, oh Deep, I loved it.

'Well, finally,' she said.

It sounded like a slap wrapped in velvet, but I pretended it was affection. I always did.

'Sorry. Figgy held me up. We were playing a game...'

'You two and your games...' Her lips twitched. Almost a smile. She stepped aside just enough to let me in. 'Come in before someone sees.'

We slipped inside, and though the click was soft, it was dramatic enough to say clearly: no one leaves unnoticed. Her room was warm, lit, and smelled of her. A jasmine.

When the door closed, she turned and kissed me. It was not welcome but urgent, a second only, take it or lose it. It landed on my mouth and vanished before I could even respond.

I stood there like an idiot, probably grinning.

'I missed you,' I breathed.

But she did not respond. Instead of sitting down, I simply strolled over to the sofa and sat down. Posed. On the armrest, back straight, ankles crossed, like she was being painted.

'I had a stupid day,' she said. 'Mum was strange. Uncle mentioned the Council. And then… well, I won.'

'Of course you did.'

I stepped closer, almost without thinking, and reached for her face. My fingers brushed her cheek.

Her eyes widened. Not from affection.

'Tonny,' she said, low and sharp. 'My makeup.'

I froze mid-cuddle. 'Sorry. I forgot. It just… looked soft.'

She narrowed her eyes, but didn't swat me away. Yet. I tried again. A hand to her hair. No. No. Bad idea.

She flinched like I'd just fired a cannon near her ear.

'Tonny!'

'I barely touched it.'

'Exactly.'

She turned her face slightly, fixing what I'd ruined with a single flick of her fingers. Perfection restored.

'So touchy today,' I muttered.

'I've been seen today. There's a difference.'

I watched her for a second. Watched how she played with the ring on her hand like she was trying to distract herself. Like if she just kept spinning it, everything would feel normal. One more time, I made contact. This time, it is less quick. Took her hand in a gentle manner.

'When Dad comes back,' I said, 'we'll get married. No ceremony. To hell with permissions. Just us.'

She looked up. Not a word, at first. Then a smile. But her eyes didn't soften.

'Really?'

'Yeah. I swear. Even if it costs me everything.'

Watching me closely, she seemed to ask if I meant it or if I only liked the drama of saying it.

Then: 'Alright.' But there was space in her voice. Cold space. A pause where warmth should have lived. 'We'll talk about it later, Tonny.'

To me, it still felt like a yes. Sort of. And then I felt it. The throb, a quiet pulse in my pocket. That cursed envelope, it buzzed like it had a deadline and no patience.

'Oh no…'

She didn't even flinch, just tilted her head.

'What now?'

'The Council. The invitation. My uncle sent a carriage to Deep. If I miss it —'

'You won't get in. Yes, yes, I know who you are.'

Slowly, she rose. Her outline in the fire, arm crossed and chin raised.

'I assume you're going then.'

'You're not going to wish me luck?'

She didn't smile, just turned.

'I don't need to. You don't need luck, Tonny. And I have a purple bath waiting. I'm busy.'

I paused by the door, looking at her over my shoulder.

'Purple bath?'

She raised an eyebrow. Dangerous.

'Can I come with you?'

Her hand moved so fast I didn't even see it. Something flew through the air.

A shoe.

I ducked, narrowly dodged it, and bolted.

'You're cheeky!' she shouted after me.

I grinned as I ran, but I swear I heard her laugh. As I disappeared down the hallway, I couldn't help it.

'I just love her,' I said to myself.

Chapter Eight
Raisin

I was ready.

Clean clothes, hair slicked back, half nervous, half focused. I was fiddling with the cuff of my sleeve like it could somehow smooth out what was inside me too. Roddy was dozing in my pocket, quiet, not making a fuss. Maybe asleep, or maybe just listening.

And around me, nothing moved. The Dustdreads passed by without a glance, because the necklace from Uncle was protecting me. It wrapped round my neck like a silent guarantee of invisibility. Breathing slower, I found that no one stared and no one felt a thing.

Then the carriage appeared out of the veil between worlds. It was not noisy or dazzling, just suddenly there. Black smooth body, almost shapeless, with a faint red shimmer rippling over the surface like the echo of a foreign sun.

When it landed, it did not creak. More like it touched the ground gently, like it did not even need to. The door opened on its own. I got in without a word, while Alan was already sitting inside. He looked just the same as when I met him in my dad's office. Neat, calm, not quite human, nor Deeper, but somehow pleasantly unsettling.

His suit did not have a speck on it, hands folded in his lap, eyes emotionless but present. He nodded. Not like a friend, more like someone who's got a lot on today.

The carriage lifted smoothly, no jolt, and started rising. Not flying though. More like gliding through layers. The Deepers around us shifted like liquid glass. First warm orange shades of Hell, then pale blue streaks of Heaven, and finally the deep grey of the Deep, but we did not touch any of it, we just passed through. And then the world tipped past the edge of the familiar. We were flying into a place that was not up or down, not even left or right. It was a realm between realms. A space set aside for higher purposes, for decisions heavier than life itself.

Beneath us a platform appeared as we slowed. It was dark, still, solid as stone, but it floated with no base beneath it. Offices surrounded us, not palaces or temples, but vast and grand, their façades smooth, their corridors empty and leading nowhere. And yet the whole place felt precise, like it all meant something. Operating as governance, it was a system, a place where life and death were managed. Where decisions were spoken aloud about things no one else even knew existed.

By one of the main entrances, the carriage came to rest. The door opened, and Alan stood up. Of course he did not say anything, just gave a small gesture to tell me to follow.

Stepping out, I caught the scent at once: paper, a freshly opened envelope, old coffee, and iron. It was strange, but I actually liked it. There was calm here, more like a hum... of thoughts, plans, decisions, air that thought before you did.

Alan walked first. I followed.

We entered the building. It started with the lift. At first it seemed ordinary, then not metal, then not square, and finally not even real. It was covered in something that looked like frozen honey, and it was literally alive.

When we stepped in, it rippled slightly, like it was checking us out from the inside. Then it gave a quiet burble, shaken us sideways and started going up. Or down? Or maybe rotating, hard to say. Every few seconds I felt like we were upside down, even though my feet stayed flat on the floor. It was honestly weird but kind of interesting too. Alan just stood calmly. He did not even grab the rail. I did. And then the lift gave me a cheeky little wink.

Yes. A lift. With an eye. Perfect.

'Bit of an odd kind of movement, this, eh?' I said quietly.

Alan did not even flinch. Just said, 'Its name is Bucket.'

'S–sorry?'

'Bucket. It was a translation error, but it stuck.'

Right. Bucket.

I could feel my throat drying up. Not from fear, just that kind of tension that settles under your tongue. Alan looked at me sideways for a moment, then asked, with the same blank expression,

'Are you nervous, Tonny?'

I swallowed.

'Yeah. I've never been to the Council before.'

Alan smiled. Actually smiled. Still calm, but something in his face shifted.

'Most of the ones sitting in there have not either.'

At that, Bucket gave a sudden metallic chuckle, a sound like coins rattling in a tin, and said, 'First time for everyone, eh? Just don't throw up on the carpet, mate. I've only just had it polished.'

I stared, eyes wide, while Alan kept on smiling as if nothing was strange about it. Then he added lightly, 'Don't say anything. He gets moody sometimes,' and gave me a quick wink.

The doors opened. Bucket gave me one last nudge in the back and spat us out into the silence. I just shuddered and drew in a deep breath.

And we entered the hall, not in that cold sort of way like the palaces of Heaven, nor in the theatrical style of Hell. It was made of stone. A bit dark and smooth, with light that did not shine from anywhere but was still there. Dim, kind of legal. On the walls there were no windows, only carvings of time, events, and old agreements. All in symbols that meant nothing to me, and at the same time, it felt like I should have known them since birth.

In the middle of the room stood a round table. Not wooden. More like it was made of something else. Looked like it had been carved from the ancient core of a star. Seven chairs around it. Tall, with backrests that rippled like they were breathing.

One chair sat empty. It was Dad's. Alan, without a word, pointed me to my place, and the sight made me ache with missing him. Realising it was no gesture of respect, I saw it for what it was: the place for the Reaper's blood. The heaviness and warmth surrounded me when I sat down, and in the silence I could hear my own thoughts.

Then I felt the looks. I couldn't see them, but I knew they were already watching. I felt good, as if I belonged, as if I mattered, like my father.

The wall puckered into a lopsided mouth and let out a snorty laugh, the kind you'd hear from a drunk uncle at a wedding, before smoothing back into stone. I tried to ignore it, but then the table gave a sharp kick into my shin. I staggered, clutching my leg, while the wood creaked like it was chuckling at its own joke.

The door opened, and the first one who came in was Satan. He looked like someone you wouldn't want to meet on a beach, because next to him your own existence would seem dull. Tall. Broad. Shoulders like gates. Blond hair tied back. Blue eyes like from a water advert. Perfect face, but no smile. He wore a leather jacket so expensive you could probably buy a planet for it. And sunglasses. Yes. Even here. Not one but two gorillas followed him, though it was hard to know if they were real or anthropomorphic. Dressed in dark suits, square-jawed and expressionless, with too many joints, they sat behind him in silence, like a shadow backup.

Satan looked at me and gave a slight nod.

'Ah, well, bless my blackened heart. Look who's sitting here. A human.'

'Deeper. I'm a Deeper,' I replied, trying not to swallow at all. 'Sir. Erm… Satan.'

'Hell's bells, I love it. That's almost cute,' he smiled, sat down opposite me, and crossed one leg over the other so lightly it looked like he weighed five kilos.

He hates me. Really hates me. Because this was Amelia's father. My Amelia.

The door opened again, and this time, God came in.

He looked... like someone who once had unlimited power, but has been leaving it on the nightstand for a few thousand years. Green robes. Golden belt. Long, dark hair, braided but a bit messy. And in his hand... a bag of raisins. Two gorillas came behind him. One helped him find his chair. The other held his hat, which he apparently didn't bring.

'Is this the room?'

'Yes, Sir,' whispered the gorilla.

'Looks like a dining hall. Will there be soup?

'No, Sir.'

'Shame.' He sat in his place, frowned at the table for a moment, and then said: 'Wood. Hm.'

It was not wood. Poor God. He needed a successor, and his head was a mess now.

And another arrival. Two big men, both in elegant grey suits, both with expressions that could be scary — if you didn't look properly. Hito and Sito. My cousins. They were the kind of lads who do not look friendly until they smile. And then suddenly you are not sure if they want to give you a hug or lift you over their head and chuck you in a river, out of love.

'Tonnyyy!' growled Hito, and gripped my shoulder like a vice.

'Look at him, he's growing up. Even wearing a suit now,' added Sito, and sat down next to me like he had been sitting there his whole life.

I just smiled, because honestly, what else was I supposed to do?

Coming in at last, my uncle arrived without little Gabriel, thank Deep. He was silent, calm, and round, his shiny shoes and feathered hat making him look exactly as he did whenever he was about to say something important. He sat down without a word. The hall was full.

All seven chairs taken. All eyes on me and I sat in the centre of the circle like the son of Death. Well, I knew now I wasn't a guest anymore.

Satan was the first to speak.

He sat comfortably, one leg over the other, hands folded on his stomach. He had not taken off his sunglasses, even though there was nothing here to reflect. His voice was calm, deep, and far too refined for someone who used to be the ruler of hellish armies.

'We've gathered because the world has stopped dying,' he said, like he was announcing a train delay. 'Hell knows I've tried. People are staying, just not ending, and as you all know, with that comes a problem.' He leaned forward slightly, like he was sharing a secret we already knew. 'Erm… Hell's rich, thanks to bad souls, of course. Until now. But now? None are coming through. We've got a Void. And that's not just a little hiccup. It's a bloody great Hole, and not only in my pocket, mind you. If it's not sealed, the whole flaming structure of Hell could topple like cheap scaffolding.'

Pause.

Satan leaned back. His body did not move much, but something in the room shivered with the shift. And right then, with the usual dry rustle of cloth, God spoke.

'Oh, wealth, of course,' he muttered, the raisin bag crackling as he shifted it in his lap. 'That's what you Hell folk are good at. Dirt, nastiness, and boasting. I suppose every kingdom has its speciality.' A raisin dropped onto the table. He stared at it. Forgot what he was saying.

Satan did not move. Just raised one eyebrow slightly and turned his head to me, like he was saying: are you seeing this?

He nodded, and God furrowed his thick brows. I only watched. Hito and Sito stared wide-eyed, and the leg of the table kept knocking against my foot. Then Satan leaned back with a smirk.

'You ought to have a successor by now. Ah, silly me, I forgot. You have not got one, have you? Poor old Heaven, left without a spare.'

Then God stood, clutching the bag of raisins in one hand while steadying his hulking guard with the other so he would not topple.

'You nasty piece of work, how dare you? Always the same with you, pointing at others. But the truth? It is you in the mirror. And for the record, I have a successor. Your Amelia, however, is not exactly the golden child who will lighten the burden of Hell.'

'You will pay for that, old man. No one speaks ill of my Amelia,' roared Satan. He sprang up, and in an instant he was looming at the ceiling. God set the raisins carefully on the table, bracing himself for the fight, and I only swallowed hard.

When God raised his hand and pointed a finger at Satan's face, he declared, 'Right then, let us see you without that ugly mouth of yours.' There was a sharp click. Whatever God had intended, it went awry. Satan's lips only flushed red for a moment before snapping back as if nothing had happened.

Satan did not flare up. Quite the opposite. He began laughing so hard he clutched his stomach.

'You know what,' he gasped between fits of laughter, 'you should try your hand at comedy. In human Hollywood they would sign you up at once. And you talk of having a successor? You have not the faintest idea how it is done. You are not capable of anything.'

With that, Satan shrank back into his usual form and dropped into his chair.

'Really?' said God, planting his hands on his hips and lifting his head high. 'Now then, it was twenty years ago, if my memory serves me... yes, yes, certainly...' He lowered his head, muttering to himself, 'Yes, certainly.'

Satan slapped his palm to his forehead. I only watched, wondering when this would end, while Hito and Sito snickered quietly.

'Ah, yes,' God went on, straightening again. 'So it was like this... well, I unzipped my trousers and —'

At that very moment my uncle leapt from his chair and cut him off.

'That is enough, you two!' he shouted. 'This is not about you. Not about Heaven, and certainly not about your trousers,' he said, shaking his head at God. Then he turned to Satan. 'Nor is it about Hell and whatever nonsense you keep going on about. For the love of Heaven, Hell, and the Deep itself, this is bigger than the pair of you!'

He swept his eyes round the room. 'Without Death, there is no order. Things stop moving. Things stop meaning anything. And if Death is not here with us, if the Dustdreads have not found him, then he must be somewhere else. In the realm of humans.'

He paused, the silence stretching. 'The humans have him. They have taken my brother. We do not know how, and we do not know why. But we do know this: the Dustdreads must be sent into their world. Into the world of people!'

Silence. Satan nodded. God was trying to stick the raisin back into the bag. My cousins, Hito and Sito, exchanged a look that clearly meant: right then, let's get to work.

Everyone agreed. Except me.

'No,' I said quietly, but everyone heard me. 'If the Dustdreads go among humans, they'll lose their minds. And the people will lose their calm. They'll panic. They'll start fearing everything. They'll start fighting back. They'll start shooting. Maybe you don't care, but they'll be damned in fear.'

The hall was silent. Brilliant. I looked down. They'd never taken humans seriously — not really. Just a punchline, or rubbish to clean up, but Dad hadn't seen them that way. And neither had I. Not that anyone here ever cared. Watching me quietly, my uncle showed no judgement, only stillness. Satan shrugged, God pushed the raisin into his pocket, and the truth was clear: people were not the priority.

Then came a sound.

Through the doorway stepped a figure who looked out of place, never meant to be there. Following came a grey-haired man, tall and thin, with a straight back, a shiny silver suit, a red bow, and a face sharply cut, dry, untouched by a smile. His eyes were Death's own, only aged, colder, and stripped bare of compassion.

'Hello everyone,' he said, all calm. 'Polite of you to be discussing my son and not invite me.'

Silence. No one moved.

God whispered, 'That's the old bloke? I thought he was dead...'

Some voice, maybe one of the gorillas, or maybe Alan, said quietly, 'Alfonzo De Death is retired.'

Alfonzo did not even look at him. He just walked through the middle of the hall like he still ran the place and stopped in front of me.

'Stand up,' he said.

I blinked.

'Sorry?'

'That chair. It is not yours. It is mine. Death is my son. You are half human, and you have not proven yourself. You have no right to sit there!'

I stood up slowly. Brilliant. Grandad.

For a second I thought about saying something, just a word to make him look at me, but I didn't. I moved to a chair a bit further away, a simple wooden one without a backrest. Everyone watched, no one spoke. I was at the centre of the room, and suddenly I was outside it.

Alfonzo sat down in the chair I had just left, and it gave a heavier sound than when I had sat there. Then he looked up.

'I love my son. And we must find him. Now. Immediately. By any means necessary.' Pause. Tension. 'The Dustdreads have already been sent. Without your permission. Yes. I did it. Because—'

'What?!' I nearly jumped out of my chair.

Of course, no one batted an eye. Alfonzo carried on like I was a bit of background noise with legs.

He raised a hand and looked across all of them.

'But it is not enough. While you sit here, the world is falling apart. There is only one option left. Until my son returns, I must take his place again. Death must be present. Otherwise the universe will not hold.'

'With all respect, Father... you retired. You passed your power to my brother. You can't just...' said my uncle.

But Alfonzo cut him off.

'This is none of your business. I am not powerless. And you dare speak to me in this manner? Did I not teach you respect?' His voice rose... sharper, colder. 'If I leave everything in your hands, the worlds will collapse. I am here to save us!'

Uncle tried again.

'Father, you were the most respected Death we ever had. But this goes against the rules. Tonny should be Death now!'

Alfonzo scoffed.

'Oh? This human?' He turned to me like I was something he had just stepped in. 'Tell me, how exactly? He possesses no power. He is the most useless human I have ever seen. You should be ashamed of even suggesting such nonsense!'

Then he laughed, cold, loud, and cruel. My uncle said nothing. Just nodded. No one else spoke. And I just sat there quietly, feeling small, knowing I was outside the circle.

Everyone, after a short pause, nodded.

My uncle looked at me. Not with pity, just the quiet knowledge that he could not stop this. My cousins did not even look at me. God was feeding a raisin to a gorilla. Satan kept tapping his fingers, eyes on the wall, like he was waiting for applause. Honestly, he could have whistled and it would've been less obvious. And Alan stood behind me. He did not move.

The council was over.

Chapter Nine
The Power of Memories

The heaviness in my chest and the necklace at my neck were with me as I sat in the carriage. Alan was next to me, and neither of us said anything. I knew that right now, in this moment, the world had closed under my feet. The carriage slid through the silence between worlds. I sat still, eyes on the glass wall, but I didn't see anything. It was more just smudges of light, mist, and somewhere in between... myself.

Alan was still quiet and stayed that way for a long time. Far too long. Then, cool as a fridge, voice low, zero blame vibes, he said, 'Why don't you go the human world and find your dad yourself?'

I blinked. 'What...? Me?'

He turned his head to me. There wasn't a smile in it, or a blade, just a plain fact.

'Who else? You are his son. You are not going to let that old man rule. If Alfonzo takes on the role of Death, your powers will never awaken. You will die as an ordinary human. And that will be it.'

I closed my eyes. 'I don't care about that, Alan. I really don't. I... I just want my dad back. Without him... I'm wrecked. Not like some tragic figure, but like something broken that no longer fits back in the box.' Alan did not move, but I could feel he was listening. 'I'm worried,' I added quietly.

Then came the answer, calm and sharp as paper.

'Exactly. And you are doing nothing about it.'

I opened my eyes. He was looking at me so directly it bothered me, and on top of that, he wasn't looking away. 'You sit. You stay quiet. You nod, but none of that will bring him back. You will not save Death with pity. And the universe does not bow to sorrow.'

I clenched my jaw. Something inside me pushed back, but I had nowhere to put it. Alan remained sitting upright, hands in his lap, and continued more quietly, intimately.

'You studied everything about the human world. You read their stories, you understand their language, you know what they eat, how they lie, how they love, how they fear. Who else could go looking for Death right there? You are his son, his successor, and maybe it is time you grew up and acted like it...'

When I looked at him, the last flame of resistance in my head went out. He was right. I knew more about the human world than any of us. It fascinated me. It scared me. It drew me in. And now it had become the doorway to the one I loved more than my own dignity.

Only one question remained.

'How?' I whispered. 'The human world is massive. I don't have a single lead.'

Alan nodded, as though he had been waiting for that exact moment. From his pocket he pulled a small metal object. It wasn't a key in the traditional sense. It was thin, dark blue, and its shape shifted depending on how you looked at it. Inside it, something bubbled, maybe light or a voice. Honestly, it was hard to tell.

'This key is from the Office of Death, the one your father gave me to look after his chamber.'

He handed it to me. I felt it with my fingers. It was cold, like a stone that had been lying at the bottom of a well. At the same time, it trembled gently in my palm, like it was breathing.

'You want to know where they took him from? We will go there together. I will open the door for you and show you what is left. And then you must decide for yourself.'

I took a breath and nodded. The carriage slowed down. Below us appeared a dark sea of buildings. But somewhere among them stood the one and only place that had been waiting for me. My palace.

Right. And there it was. The only door in the whole palace I had never been allowed to enter. Not even by mistake. Not even when I was little and had tried to sneak along the walls, in a breath that didn't want to exist. A door without a name. Without a handle. Without anything to suggest it could even be opened.

Now I stood there. Next to me, of course, Alan. He was holding a key in his hand, one without teeth, and yet it unlocked something. I had no idea why I was nervous, but I was. Not from fear, more from that strange kind of tension that settled behind your breastbone when you were about to open something you'd imagined your whole life. And mostly... I was curious. I didn't know what to expect, but I knew that once I went through, nothing would ever be the same.

Alan inserted the key. It was a bit strange. There wasn't a click, just that gentle yes the world gave when you let it breathe. The door gave way. Alan went in first, which I didn't like, but I didn't deal with it. I simply followed him.

Inside it was no room at all, only a system, like the dark heart of a galaxy or the digital soul of the universe. Beneath our feet stretched a surface that kept changing shape. First a map, then geometry, then just a whisper under the fingers. When I looked up, above my head there were... thoughts. Lights without a source, and yet they were alive. They moved by rules known only to themselves.

And in the middle of it all, the Web.

It was the Death Control Centre. A circle made of layers, rings, belts and currents. Each represented a different plane: time, body, soul, place, cause, even that invisible point between exhale and silence. Now I understood why this room had been forbidden.

Alan spoke to me, a bit quiet, but firm.

'Death could never be in one place. Not in two either. Not in a thousand.' He pointed at the currents of light rotating around us. 'Here it was distributed. Here it multiplied. Every day, every second. What you met outside were just its fragments, images. Projections.' Above us, one of the light rings went out. Alan raised his hand to it and the image settled. 'The core consciousness stayed here. This room... was its anchor. The core. And from here, it sent out parts of itself. To every death. Every ending had its own Death, but they were all him.'

I looked at it.

And suddenly it all started to make sense. Why he was never tired. Why he never slept. Why he came for the old man and for the woman on the same day, the same minute, on opposite sides of the world.

He didn't walk. He spread.

'It was like a heart and a beat,' Alan said. 'The system stayed here, but the action was scattered. He was more than just a person. He was... a function. And that function is now missing.'

He placed his palm on one of the rings and immediately the whole space around us changed. The lights that had been circling in web-like patterns pulled back into silence, as if the whole system was waiting for another command. Everything quietened. The Web withdrew into a single point.

Right in front of us, an image began to slowly form, not like a hologram, but like a transparent layer of reality, which gently peeled away from space and showed what had been.

A street appeared. Night city. The lights of street lamps reflected on the wet road, and now and then a drop of rain landed on stone. At the kerb stood a trio: a man in a suit, a woman with a bag in her hand, between them a child holding their hands. And one younger woman, or girl.

And just a few metres further stood a tall figure in a suit. It was... my father.

Alan looked at the image without blinking and spoke quietly, without unnecessary gestures.

'Here he appeared for the last time. London. Crowley Road. This was the last known location.'

The image blurred slightly, but didn't disappear, as if it was trying to stay a little longer. I felt my chest tighten. That view wasn't just a display. A trace it was. This is where it all began: a caught breath. In space, the picture stayed put.

'And then?' I whispered.

Alan didn't answer right away. He was quiet for a moment. Then he said, 'After that, there was no more record. Absolutely nothing, as if someone cut the cord. Did not kill him, did not stop him, just cut him out.'

I looked at that place. The street looked usual, like a million others. Yet something had happened there that no one knew how to repeat. I took the key out of my pocket. It pulsed, faintly, but alive.

'So… I'm supposed to go there?'

'Yes.'

'You sure?'

'Yes.'

I looked at Alan's face as he stepped to a table, opened a narrow black box, and took out something I'd only seen in books. Cash? Yes… real British pounds.

'You'll need this,' he said. 'People have a strange relationship to values. This seems to them like proof of reality.'

I remembered that when I was little, Dad had shown me a similar one. He had told me that money wasn't important, but without it, people couldn't survive.

Alan tossed the bundle of money in front of me. I looked at it, and then it came.

'You must follow the rules,' he began.

I raised my hand. 'No, Alan. Not for me. I know the rules!'

I looked into his eyes, and suddenly I felt it all rise inside me, like wind before a storm. I had studied this all my life. While others wasted their lives, I got lost in human maps, films, speech, behaviour, memory. While someone else was solving how exactly to guide a soul into the light, I was reading what 'light' actually meant to them.

I knew how restaurant's worked. I knew why they argued about a parking space. I knew how to buy a ticket, how to call a taxi, how to spot a lie in someone's eyes. Because I had learned their words, their phrases, their silence, I was not afraid of people. I was ready for that world through knowledge, not strength or experience. And mostly, I had a reason.

Alan didn't say anything for a while, he nodded slightly.

'Alright. Just remember one thing.'

He paused, his voice softer. It wasn't a sentence he said often. 'If you are in trouble, tell them clearly and very loudly who you are! Without fear. You are Death's son. A prince. An heir! And even though you are half human, that will not disappear.'

I nodded. 'Yeah. Right.' It was strange to hear it, as if someone had given me a title for the first time that actually meant something. I smiled. 'I don't need a guidebook. I have my reason, and I'm going to find him. Whatever it takes!'

Alan bowed, stepping over to one of the breaks, pressing his palm against an engraving that looked just like a shadow in the wall.

There was a soft click. The stone beneath our feet slowly slid away. And beneath it was a mirror, but it wasn't silver. It was darker and matte. It moved, not like water, not like smoke either, but like memory.

'This gate,' said Alan, 'is one of those that do not open for the body. Only for consciousness.'

I stopped.

'Wait… you mean I won't go… physically?'

'No. You will go through. Entirely… but what pulls you through is not a path. It is a memory of you.'

'Meaning what?'

Alan finally smiled at me, just slightly.

'You are half human. And a human is born from the memory of others. That is the only way to get into their world without an invitation. Memories of you do not exist in that world yet, but I shall plant one there. Just one. In the mind of a child.'

I just stood for a moment. I didn't understand it all, but at the same time, it was beautifully logical.

'So… somewhere in London, a child who's never seen me will remember me, and that'll pull me inside?'

'Exactly, once you are there… breathe slowly. Do not look up. And do not forget who you are.'

I stepped up to the gate, looked into its darkness.

'I'm coming for you, Dad. Hold on,' I whispered and jumped.

At first there was nothing. And then there was too much of everything.

A fall.

But not having a body. Not able to breathe. Without a plan. I felt something break. Not my bones, but the very idea of 'me'. Colours that had no names, smells that belonged to nothing, and thoughts that didn't belong to me. For a moment, I was in someone else's head. I saw a school desk, crayons, a drawing of a dog.

And then...

As if it tore open. As if someone remembered me, someone who'd never seen me, but still knew me. That image grabbed me. It reached for me, and I had a body with weight, skin, and lungs that breathed. Muscles that pulled against the asphalt.

I was there. Really.

My lungs hurt from breathing. British weather: wet and chilly. Somewhere in the distance, a dog barked. I was lying on a pavement. A real one. Wet cobblestones. A streetlamp flickering, and right next to me, a sign: Crowley Road. Lifting my head, I saw a grey sky above, poised to hide something. I felt the warmth of the money in my pocket.

Ah... London. The human world.

Chapter Ten
Into the City

At the edge of the road I stood, an umbrella in one hand and myself in the other, because this was a moment.

I know how it works. People raise a hand, shout 'Taxi!' and right after that, their life changes. I've read it a hundred times, of course, I studied taxis: types, habits. I even had a whole subchapter on cultural differences between New York and London hailing styles.

So when I raised my hand with confident, almost like in a film, I was sure I'd done it right. And nearly smacked someone with my new umbrella, the one I bought for five quid on the corner. But never mind. This is what I'd always wanted.

To call a taxi. Seriously.

'Taxi!' I called out, almost too dramatically, but the handbook said it should be like that. There was a hint of pride in it. I was ready to tell the driver exactly where I wanted to go, whip out the address, and look like someone who does this every day. And guess what?

It stopped. It actually stopped. Black, shiny, with an orange sign on the roof. Exactly like it's meant to be. I opened the door, and the smell of cheap pine air freshener hit me in the face like an invitation to life.

I got in. My heart jumped. I was sitting in a taxi. Me. Tonny. In a taxi. In the human world. The driver turned to me, smiling in that way only middle-aged Indian men with twenty years' experience and zero patience can smile. He had a turban, thick eyebrows, and a gold chain across his belly like a golden grin that forgot when to stop.

'So, where to, boss?'

'Into the city,' I said with a tone that was meant to sound professional.

'London's all city,' he replied, all cheerful. 'That's like saying you want to go into the water. But alright. You comfy there, sir?'

'Yes,' I said. 'I've never been in one of these... I mean... often. Like... I know it. From studying.'

'Ah,' he nodded, in the tone of someone who's heard worse. 'These days everyone's a bit foreign, innit.'

The taxi started moving. It pushed me back into the seat, but only slightly. Enough to make me feel like I was in a film, not enough to admit it out loud. I took Roddy out of my pocket and set him on my thigh so he could see too, or at least hear. He senses vibration more than light.

'Here we go, mate,' I whispered, 'off to the core.'

'If by core you mean a busy street full of accidents and shopping bags, then congrats. Great pick,' Roddy muttered.

The driver glanced back slightly, but from the look on his face he thought I was talking on the phone. Which suited me just fine.

'So, sir,' the driver said with a grin, 'first day in London? You've got the look. Tourist. Or on the run. That's half the city nowadays.'

'No, I... I work here.' I straightened up a bit. 'I'm... actually... a specialist in transitions.'

'In what?'

'In death.'

The silence held with only wipers moving. Then he laughed, uncertain whether to stop or keep going.

'Right, good one. So you've got a lot on your plate these days then, eh? Hospital work?'

'Not exactly... in the hospital. More... above it.'

He paused. Looked me over again in the rear-view mirror.

'Well... look. Honestly? Nothing surprises me anymore. Last week I had a bloke swear time was following him. Literally. Said it was growing out of his back. But you... you look like someone who genuinely believes he belongs here.'

I smiled. A bit nervously, but still.

'I know it sounds mad. But I'm Death's son. Really. And I've come to find him.'

Silence again.

Then he cleared his throat.

'Well look, I don't really know much about this stuff, yeah? But things have been acting weird this past week. Accidents every day. People jumping in front of trains and... not dying. Hospitals are packed. My brother-in-law had a stroke. Brain's gone, they said. But the body's still going. Three days now and guess what... he is breathing. Just like that.' He shook his head. 'And then some preacher said Death disappeared because we didn't deserve him. So... if you're Death's son, then... welcome back, sir.'

His smile shifted. It was careful. Like when you're not sure if you're driving a prophet, or a nutter.

'Thanks,' I said.

'St. Elwick's Hospital, right? They say that's where the strangest bit started. Apparently someone spoke to a shadow there. Someone who came for a patient, but then... vanished.'

'Yes. There.'

He was already turning into the street. Above the hospital hung a billboard for vitamins, and underneath it the slogan read:

'You'll survive with us. Literally.'

Before we even made it to the junction, the driver started swearing.

'Oh, you're having a laugh! What's that bloke doing!'

I lifted my head from Roddy. Right in front of us, standing squarely in the middle of the road, was a man. He was soaked, hunched over, wearing a coat even bin men would have refused to take back. Then, with no expression and no warning, he stepped forward.

Right in front of the car.

'Oh, for fu-!'

The driver slammed the brakes. Tyres screeched. Everything lurched. I smacked my head against the front seat. Roddy hit the dashboard. A thud followed. I froze. The driver kept both hands on the wheel. And then the man got up. Slowly, he brushed off his coat, checked his shoulder and started shouting.

'Oh, come on! Still nothing?! I'm done with this bloody city! When's it going to end already?!' He turned towards us, furious like a customer who had been served a cold coffee, and yelled, 'That was meant to be the finale. Do you get that? A direct hit! And me? Nothing. Nothing!'

He gasped for breath, from pure frustration. Then he walked off, disappearing around the corner as if he had simply got the wrong street. Inside the taxi, it was so quiet I could swear I heard my moral compass slowly backing away from the scene.

Roddy rolled back into my lap. 'Well... at least now you're only the second weirdest person around.'

The driver cleared his throat.

'See? That's what I mean. That's London now. Every bloody day. People've stopped believing in death, but they still want to leave.'

He started driving again.

I sat there, quiet, breathing, and it really hit me how serious this was. This wasn't a glitch. There was a world that was stuck.

'St Elwick's,' the driver said, slightly frowning but with that usual resignation you get from people who had already seen enough weirdness in one day not to be thrown off by a lad in a dark coat. 'God bless you, sir. Twenty-one pounds, please.'

Cash was passed over, the door closed, and there was nothing left but standing there. Not because I was about to walk, but precisely because I wasn't. Because of the air. I wanted to take in the air. Standing on the pavement like someone who had just been born again, I took a deep breath, filled my lungs and nose with it as if I was breathing in more than just oxygen.

And maybe I was. It was London, after all. The real wet, dirty and alive one. Ah… I loved it. I could smell kebab smoke, bus fumes, raindrops hitting window ledges and smashing onto the pavement. To me, it smelled like… life.

'Yeah,' I said to myself, more to say it than to make a point. 'We don't have this at home.'

Because in the Deep, breathing was different. There, you inhaled clauses, conditions, exceptions to rules written before light existed. There, air had structure. Here? Here, it had a soul.

Roddy took a quick look out of my pocket. Not even a second. Not overt. Probably keeping an eye on me.

'I know,' I told him. 'I look a bit emotional. But listen, when you've spent your whole life reading about something you thought you'd never taste, and someone finally gives it to you, you can't just brush it off.'

Roddy stayed silent. Maybe he approved, maybe he was just staring at the pavement, maybe asleep. I gave him a gentle puff of breath, that old gesture of trust I had held onto even when the Deep was choking me. Then I slipped him back into my inside pocket. Another breath was taken by me. This time, there is a little less flair to it. More responsible in certain ways.

I looked up straight at the building ahead.

St Elwick's hospital.

It was meant to look like a place that saved lives, but in that moment, it felt more like a monument. Something that still stood, but already knew it served a different purpose than it was built for.

In the direction of the entrance, I walked. Certainly not in a heroic manner, and certainly not in a hurry; merely with intent. Because in this world, I had one advantage. I knew what I was looking for.

The doors hissed shut behind me and I stepped inside.

Weird.

There was no one in the lobby. A stillness before the storm that is not empty. More along the lines of everyone having been paid and gone home empty. The floor was shiny, it looked like someone had spilled tea and left it there. The reception desk was overturned. Someone had clearly been searching for something they didn't find, or maybe found something they weren't meant to.

In the corner was a crumpled flu leaflet. Above it, a sign read, 'Health is a choice.' Yeah, that didn't hold up anymore. I thought about calling out, 'Hello?', but it felt daft. Talking into an empty space always makes you feel like an idiot. I was about to leave.

Then I heard something. It wasn't a voice, neither a scream, but a soft rustle, more like the sound of plastic being stuffed into a carrier bag. So I followed it. A man was crouching around the corner, just outside the pharmacy's kicked-in doors. An older one. Hair was messy and lengthy. The green parka jacket looks like a relic from a better time.

He was sitting there calmly, stuffing boxes into a Tesco bag. No panic, just routine. I stopped and watched him for a moment to see if he'd notice me. He didn't. He was lost in his own world, one where rules didn't seem to apply.

Into my pocket I reached, drawing out a few notes. British, though I had no idea how much, and honestly, I didn't care. 'Hi,' I said. Not threatening. Not friendly.

Just... hi.

He looked up. Eyes bloodshot. Face like someone who had been outside for seven nights straight, but he didn't flinch. He just gave me a once-over and went back to loading pills into the bag.

'There's no one here anymore,' he said. 'They don't care. No one cares about anything now.'

'You stayed behind?'

'Me? Nah. I'm just picking through what's left.' He shrugged. 'No one's dying, but everyone's gone. So what? I'll take something before the rats do.'

I handed him the money. He didn't say thank you, he said something else.

'You know what's the worst?' he said quietly. 'It's not that people don't go. It's that they still look like they're waiting.'

I raised an eyebrow.

'Waiting for what?'

'For someone to come back and turn it off. Maybe for someone like you.'

'Like me? You know who I am?'

'What I know or don't know doesn't matter. What matters is, they're waiting. And you're in the wrong place.'

'I don't understand. I'm just... anyway, I'm looking for —'

'He isn't here. Find the girl.'

It was then that he turned to the drugs. Exactly like that, he vanished without a trace. Never again did he say a word. The only thing that remained was his clothing, which was rumpled on the ground.

Chapter Eleven
Hey, London

I was walking because I could, because this was the world I'd spent my whole life reading about, and now I could finally walk through it with no obligation, no escort, and no rules. Along the pavement I went, skipping over cracks in the stone like traps, humming a tune from the taxi.

I didn't even know what it was, but I felt like singing. 'La la… heeeey London, I'm aliiiive…'

Yeah, it sounded out of tune, but I didn't care. People looked at me. Someone stopped. Someone else sped up. A group of teenagers laughed, and one of them filmed me on his phone. I felt like waving, so I did. 'I'm a tourist!' I called out to them with a grin. 'First day on Earth! You've got brilliant rain here!'

Someone threw a coin at me, thinking I was mad, and maybe they were right, but today I didn't mind. Took it as a donation to the cause. I spent it on a cup of coffee from a dingy little stall because, naturally, I had to. I wasn't on holiday. I had a mission and lives at risk, but I tried coffee anyway. It burned and tasted of ash, yet it was the best I had ever had.

Stopping by the river, I looked up at one of those massive, historic stone bridges. Beneath it, the water moved, grey and sluggish, as though it had lost all interest in going anywhere.

Into the current I stared, and only then did I notice the people. A line of them stood along the bridge railings. Maybe ten, maybe twenty. Men and women, young and old, holding hands. Some were crying, some were singing. At first, I thought it was a protest, some kind of happening, or a performance.

Something was heard by me. Quite quiet. Even less than sharp. The world is nothing more than a single word, thrown into it like a coin into a drain.

'Now.'

Therefore they jumped. Like gravity owed them something and they'd come to collect. One after another, or maybe all at once. Hard to tell. Time gets weird when you're watching people disappear off a bridge.

I didn't move. My shoes stayed stuck to the pavement, like they'd decided this was their final form. I still had the coffee in my hand, lukewarm and probably terrible, after only one sip.

My brain scrambled to catch up. Was this real? Was this happening? Was I supposed to do something? Spoiler alert: I did nothing. After that, there was complete stillness. Nobody made a scream. There was no loud splash that echoed back across the water. Instead, there was only the dull and unpleasant sound of something hitting the river. It did not sound like the dramatic noises you hear in films. This sound was heavier, and it felt final.

Then I saw movement.

From the edge of the bridge, I could only see a small part of the river, but it was enough to make me uneasy. A figure slowly began to rise from the water. The way it moved was strange, as if standing up was something it had not done for a very long time. Then another figure appeared, and then another. They were not moving quickly or smoothly, but they were definitely rising from the water.

There was no blood in the water. Instead, the bodies slowly began to rise again. At last, someone on the bridge shouted out, and the sound of their voice carried a feeling of disappointment.

'No! Why not?! Why doesn't it work?!'

I turned. People were panicking now, running, screaming, scattering in every direction. Someone dropped a bag and took off down the street. Sirens came from both directions. These were not the kind of police officers people were familiar with. Black vans pulled up, and from them stepped men wearing helmets and heavy armour. They carried weapons and spoke sharply into their radios, giving urgent orders to secure the area, isolate the zone, and allow no contact or approach.

The reaction of the crowd was immediate. Many began to run, some held up their phones to capture what was happening, and others lowered their heads in prayer. Everyone understood that the situation unfolding before them was far from ordinary. I stayed where I was, unable to move. It did not feel like simple fear or pain; it felt instead as though the very fabric of the world was beginning to break apart.

Then, from the water, one of the women who had leapt into the river and somehow survived began to raise herself. She lifted her head slowly, and her eyes searched through the gathering until they found me. Her look was steady and direct. It was not the casual glance of a passer-by nor the frightened stare of someone caught in chaos. It was the deliberate recognition of someone who could see I did not belong in that place.

Her gaze held mine, and I could not turn away. It was not because of the colour of her eyes, nor even because of the way she looked at me, but because of the knowledge they carried. In that moment, I realised she understood exactly who I was.

Before I had the chance to respond, a sudden shove from the side broke the connection.

'Move it, clown!'

There was a sudden jolt as someone's shoulder struck mine. I turned quickly, half-prepared to apologise and half-prepared to lash out. Standing in front of me was a young man who could not have been more than twenty years old. He wore a black hoodie, the hood pulled low over his face as though he wanted to appear mysterious. In one hand he carried a baseball bat, holding it casually, as if he were on his way to play a very rough game of rounders. Yet it was not the bat that caught my attention. It was the wide grin spread across his face.

It stretched too wide, teeth on full display, like he'd just won something awful and couldn't wait to show it off. There was something far too pleased with itself about that face. That was the kind of smile you wear when you know what happens next and you've decided to enjoy the mess.

Then he laughed. It was full, warm, and completely out of place, like he'd remembered the best joke in the world and didn't care that no one else was laughing. He ran into the road without turning around. He was not avoiding or pausing; he was going straight ahead, as if he were after a bus that did not exist.

Right towards the police van. Someone shouted. Officer voice. Northern, loud, trying to sound in control.

'Oi, you. Stop right there.'

He didn't. Of course he didn't. He raised a middle finger like it was a royal wave and kept running.

And then came the hit.

He slammed into the front of the van with a sound that didn't belong in the real world. His body bounced, folded, flipped, and crashed to the ground in a way that made everyone nearby instantly rethink their life choices.

There was a terrible crack. It was not the sound of a twig snapping or a plate breaking, but the sort of noise that reached the body before the ears, sinking into the spine like a warning. People around me screamed. Something fell to the ground, and a phone landed with its camera still recording. One of the officers stepped forward with narrowed eyes, looking as though he was half-expecting to see blood and half-hoping for it.

But the boy moved. He sat up slowly, as though it were an ordinary Sunday morning and everything that had just happened was part of a plan only he understood. Tilting his head from side to side, he stretched his neck until a sharp pop echoed out, like the cork of a champagne bottle, except far more disturbing.

He blinked. And then he laughed again, like none of it mattered. Like getting hit by a van was just the opening act.

'HAHA! THAT WAS AMAZING! KNOW WHAT I'M TRYING TOMORROW? A TRAIN!'

He stood, wobbling slightly. Took a theatrical bow. The officers just stood there, frozen. And him? He started spinning the bat in circles and singing: 'DEATH'S ON HOLIDAY, BABY! AND IT BLOODY LOVES ME!'

He thrust his hips, mimed a gun to his head, and then pointed straight at me. 'You! You saw that, didn't you?! This is our world now! No rules! No punishment! No end! So what d'you say? You in?'

I didn't answer because I couldn't. Because while he laughed, I heard something else. That cracking sound of the world, that quiet pressure when reality says: We weren't supposed to do this.

'You're not one of us, are you?' he said, a bit quieter, closer now. He squinted, and then he did it. He flicked me in the middle of the forehead. 'Weird... it's like you've got something extra,' he muttered, blinking, then shrugged.

'Ah well. Sooner or later, we all join in. Just gotta wait till it hurts enough.'

He turned and wandered off, still laughing, blood trickling down from his forehead.

He didn't care. I just stood there, holding a cup of coffee, and suddenly the bitterness felt pointless. I moved away from the bridge. There was no reason for me to leave. I did so because when someone looks at you from the river like they know everything about you, it is best to turn your back on them and act like you do not know anything.

I walked along the rails. The coffee cup was too cold to drink from now on, but I didn't want to throw it away. Because it was mine. Because the man who sold it had a beard and a dirty apron and asked me if I was 'local' — and I, for the first time in my life, said, 'Actually, yeah.'

London had its own beat that I could feel under my feet. A little broken and tense, but still living This was exactly how I'd pictured it. The streets, the paving stones, the noise, the air smelling of rain, cigarettes and newspapers. When I was a child, I used to draw this place and even labelled every part of it. Now I had finally arrived, but there was no map in my hands and no one to tell me where I should go.

It was… brilliant. And a bit terrifying.

A faint buzz came from my pocket. It was Roddy. I took him out.

'Hey. Slow it down, Tonny. You're elevating your heart rate.'

'I'm excited,' I smiled.

'I know. You're doing little hops. It's not cool. But I get it.'

I laughed.

People around me were staring. Maybe because of the laugh, maybe because Roddy's eyes were glowing like tiny torches.

A kid pointed.

'Mum, look! That little man's talking!'

His mum pulled him away.

I tucked Roddy back into my pocket, not all the way, just so his head was still sticking out.

'You should be asleep,' I said.

'You should be careful,' he replied, starting to blink slowly.

I smiled quietly to myself, feeling a strange little warmth at the simple idea that we were both here, together, walking through a world that wasn't ours but maybe didn't mind too much that we were visiting.

Down a quieter side street I turned, grateful for the hush that came, the thinning crowds, the calmer air. It felt like stepping out of a noisy room and finding, unexpectedly, the soft hum of silence waiting on the other side.

Then, almost immediately, I felt something, just a slight brush against the back of my neck, so faint I might have imagined it. I didn't react at first because it was easy enough to dismiss as accidental, someone passing too close without noticing.

But then it happened again, this time with more intention, a quick bump to my shoulder accompanied by an overly casual voice mumbling, 'Sorry,' in a tone that sounded rehearsed, too smooth to be genuine.

Almost instantly, Roddy lit up, his frantic voice bursting into life inside my pocket. 'Hey! Contact! Unknown hand! This isn't in protocol.'

Then, rapidly, he fell silent.

My hand moved automatically toward the pocket where he had been, and my fingers slipped inside to find nothing there. My heart gave a sudden, painful squeeze. 'No... no, no, no...' I whispered to myself, already checking every pocket, every part, even the small hidden pouch I'd carefully sewn into the lining of my coat, the one that was supposed to be secure, holding money I rarely needed, but always felt safer having.

Everything was gone. Roddy, the money, my entire sense of security, really. It was as though someone had carefully reached into my chest and pulled out the very thing that kept me steady.

Roddy had spoken. He had flashed bright and talked loud, which meant whoever took him had seen him clearly and thought nothing of it. He probably just looked at the little glowing thing and thought, casually, 'Oh, that looks valuable. I'll take that.'

He had stolen him. Stolen Roddy from me.

From me. Tonny. The Prince of the Deep. Son of Death. Someone who, supposedly, could predict and understand people better than they understood themselves. There is probably a special brand of coffee in hell for people like that thief, always lukewarm, slightly burnt, and served without sugar or mercy.

My breathing was shallow now, not from fear exactly, but from a careful attempt not to let the panic take hold. I knew if I let myself breathe too deeply, something inside me would come loose and shatter completely. Clever and prepared, that's who I was supposed to be. Yet here I stood, robbed in broad daylight, at five in the afternoon on a public street in the world of humans.

Congratulations to all of us.

But then something in the atmosphere changed slightly, not the sound, not the rain, but the feeling of being watched differently.

I turned slowly and saw a girl standing quietly nearby. She had clearly been there for some time, waiting patiently for me to notice her. Her brown hair was still damp from the rain, pale strands clinging to her forehead and cheeks, and she didn't move to brush them away. She seemed entirely unconcerned with how she looked, and strangely, that only made her seem more perfectly suited to the moment.

She appeared around twenty, maybe slightly older, but her eyes held the kind of stillness you usually see only in someone who's carried more weight than they've ever been asked to bear, yet still found a way to stand calmly beneath it.

She stepped toward me slightly and said, in a quiet, certain voice, 'I knew I'd find you.' It wasn't dramatic, it was simply stated as a fact, as though it had always been inevitable.

I stared at her, and slowly, like water seeping into cloth, the full reality of what had happened sank in again. Roddy, missing from my pocket, my hands empty, that hollow feeling in my chest where something more than just a companion had been ripped away. Not my heart, exactly, more like home, or safety, or something else equally irreplaceable.

'He spoke,' I said, my voice sounding oddly sharp and out of place in the quiet street. 'Whoever took him saw him. They must have seen him, right?'

She didn't answer immediately, but gave a small nod, barely noticeable. A gesture that said she was listening, even if she didn't yet understand fully.

'I left him exposed, wide open. I...' My words faltered and I rubbed my forehead, not because I was trying to think clearly but because it was the only thing preventing me from collapsing right there in front of her. I wasn't going to cry, not now, not here. This wasn't the moment when everything fell apart. At least, not yet.

Then I noticed something small in her hand, not Roddy, not any kind of weapon, just a slip of paper that was soaked through, the ink smudged from rain.

Her eyes rose to meet mine again, the calmness in them unshaken, the steadiness firm, and when she spoke it was quiet. 'He was small. And he was laughing.'

I stared at her blankly. 'Who?'

'The one in your pocket, the one with the blinking eyes,' she said softly. 'I saw him earlier, even before someone took him.'

My breath caught slightly, disbelief filling my chest. She had seen him. She knew he existed, even before he was stolen.

'And you didn't say anything?' I asked, unable to hide a slight accusation in my voice.

'I didn't want to scare you,' she replied calmly. 'You looked like someone who believed he had everything under control.'

That hurt more deeply than I'd expected it to, possibly because it was true. I had believed exactly that. 'I did have everything under control,' I insisted, my voice sounding weak even to myself.

She moved a step closer, unfazed by the rain that continued to fall gently around us. She seemed oddly at peace with it, as though it understood her and she understood it.

'What's your name?' she asked.

'Tonny,' I said, and then added softly, almost as though confessing something shameful, 'Son of Death.'

She didn't laugh, didn't react with surprise or skepticism. She just nodded again, calmly, as if I had merely confirmed something she already knew. 'I know,' she said.

Then she glanced around, carefully observing the street as though sensing something that hadn't yet appeared. 'It's not safe here. We should go.'

I didn't ask where. I wasn't sure it even mattered, really, because in that moment, the only thing I knew for certain was that I wanted to follow her.

She was the only person in this weird, crazy world who did not think I was crazy. She may have been the first person I did not mind being sad in front of.

Chapter Twelve
Report a Theft

We walked side by side. I was glancing around with the wide-eyed eagerness of someone who had just tasted candyfloss for the first time and then found a thorn hidden inside it.

'So... the police is the first logical step. Theft, report, official statement, records. I know how this works. I've seen it. I've studied it. I know what stations look like, the rules, the process, and how they're supposed to react. I know what I'm doing.'

Mostly, I was talking to myself. No words were spoken by her. Throughout the streets, she simply continued walking and directing me. There were no comments, no nods, and no sound at all, only that quiet kind of attention which feels more genuine than any quick reply of 'yes, you're right'. 'Hey... we never actually said your name,' I said, somewhere between two raindrops sliding down my face like lost tears that hadn't made it.

After a small pause, she gave me a fleeting look.

'Lucy.'

There was no extra detail, only the name. I nodded and said nothing more, letting the name fall into that strange silence stretching between us, a silence that suddenly felt wider than I had expected.

A few steps later, we reached the station. I recognised it instantly. The façade, the typical entrance, the familiar sign. Only the sign was hanging crooked, the window frames were scratched to bits, and one of the windows had been smashed completely. By the door stood two men who looked more like cloakroom attendants from a dodgy pub than actual officers. They looked far too tired.

Lucy stopped.

'I'll go in. Report it. Theft, talking artefact, wallet... I'm the victim. Makes sense, right?'

She smiled.

'Alright. But...' she nodded at the bench beneath the overhang, 'I'll wait here.'

I blinked.

'You're not coming in with me?'

'No. It's your turn now.'

And she sat down. Her wet coat stuck to the wooden bench, but she didn't seem to notice or care. I looked at her again. Then at the station. Then at the sign. And I went in.

The first thing that hit me wasn't the smell or the light. It was the tension. It hung in the air and clung to your skin before your brain even registered where you were. It was everywhere. In the walls, in the floor, in the shouting, the crying, the arguing, and in those people just sitting in silence, staring into nothing as though someone had unplugged their souls and forgotten to plug them back in.

The sign at reception was tilted. Someone had slapped a piece of tape over it with 'DO NOT KNOCK' written in all capital letters, but still, every other person slammed their fist against it.

A woman nearby was screaming into her phone.

'I'M TELLING YOU HE'S DEAD! I'M LOOKING RIGHT AT HIM!'

Next to her, a man in a blood-stained hoodie was clutching a teddy bear and smiling. Behind the plexiglass sat a female officer who wasn't even pretending to be working. She was scribbling something on her own hand with a pen. Right. Maybe not quite like the books, but still, it was an institution. A place people go when they need justice.

Stepping up to the desk, I adjusted my collar and spoke clearly and properly, just as I had practised.

'Good afternoon. I'd like to report a theft. A device of exceptional value was stolen from me, along with cash. The individual made physical contact. I can provide a description.'

The officer at the desk looked up. His eyes were red and heavy with exhaustion. He stared at me for a moment... not with interest, but as if trying to figure out whether I was even real. Then he looked back down at his coffee cup as though it were a more urgent case than I was.

'Another wizard?' he muttered.

'I'm not a wizard. I'm a prince. Son of Death.'

A few heads turned. Someone laughed.

The officer simply snorted through his nose.

'Yeah, we had two yesterday. Claimed they were the children of God. One of them had paper wings.'

Heat rose in my cheeks. No, that wasn't me. I wasn't some lunatic with delusions. I knew who I was, with laws, origins, and a purpose.

'So we're not writing anything up, Mister Deathy?' he asked, raising an eyebrow as if this were all part of some running joke.

'I'm telling you, I've been robbed—'

'Yes, yes, every day someone walks in here claiming that something has gone missing. Do you know what we're really missing? Capacity, patience, and storage. So the answer is no. No report, no forms. Cheers.'

And in that moment, something inside me snapped. It was not anger or violence that rose up, but a deep and heavy shame. A humiliation that seeps all the way into your bones.

'I'm Tonny! Prince of the Deep! Son of Death! And this is how you treat me?!' I shouted, because there was no way not to shout.

'Yes, yes. And I'm Jesus, retired,' he muttered, waving me off like I was an advert he hadn't asked for.

I can't explain why I did it, or even how. All I knew in that moment was that it felt like the only thing left to me. I struck him, not with full force but deliberately, so he would understand that I refused to be ignored. It was like hitting a statue that pretends you do not exist. For a second everything went silent, then the shouting began, and moments later I was forced face down on the floor with a knee pressing into my back as handcuffs snapped shut around my wrists.

'You're under arrest. Assaulting an officer. Congratulations, Your Highness!'

They locked me in a cell, which was damp and smelled unpleasant. I leant against the wall, slowly slid down to the floor, and only then did I realise that this was my very first day in the world of humans.

And I had a brand. Alone here without Roddy, without powers, without anything at all, there were only the bars and a name nobody recognised. The ground was rough concrete, dirty and scratched, with the smell of lost dreams and damp socks hanging in the air. Lowering myself onto it, I leaned my head against the wall and closed my eyes, though not for long, because there was little peace to be found in that darkness.

'Brilliant, Tonny. Really brilliant. Well done. Your first day among humans, and you already had a record. Congratulations. All you needed now was a skull tattoo, and you could join some gang down in the underground.'

I squinted upwards. Bars. Cold light. Beside me sat a bigger man in a grey vest who smelled like a school cafeteria. He looked like he had long since stopped believing in anything. Maybe even in life itself. Hard to tell. I sat there, feeling as if my bones were cracking... not literally, but as if something was missing, something I might never find again.

There was silence, but not the comforting kind. This silence pressed between your ribs. It carried a hidden warning, whispering that you might stay here forever.

'I honestly don't know what to do,' I whispered. 'I kept thinking about how stupid an idea it was... coming here. Especially alone. Humans... they're just different.'

'Yeah, I believe you,' he grunted. 'I'm human. And even I'm different.'

'No, sorry. Didn't mean to offend.'

'You didn't.'

We fell silent again.

Then he asked softly, as if afraid: 'What's it like... down there?'

'It's not down there. Or up there. But... actually, it's pretty great. It's my home.'

'Yeah. Everyone loves their home, but I'm asking more about Hell. That's what's waiting for me when Death comes.'

'Listen... it's nice there. Just not for you humans.'

'Nothing new there. But thanks for trying.'

'You won't remember your life anyway. So don't worry. Help me get out of here, and I'll put in a good word. I've got a cousin there.'

'A cousin? You're not lying?'

'I promise. I'm a prince, and when I promise something, I keep it.'

'Fine. Then it's simple. Call someone, like family. A mate. Anyone who could come to get you.'

I lifted my head. 'Well, you're a genius.'

And there I stood, leaning against the bars with a man who was about to die but believed me. For a moment, the world seemed a bit less lost.

I straightened up. 'I want to contact my grandfather. Nathaniel Whitlow. Hanover Gardens. Under law 17b/88, first-line relatives have the right to facilitated visits if no formal charges have been made. You know that, right?'

The policeman stared at me for a moment. 'You're making that up.'

'Maybe. Maybe not... but it sounds official enough, doesn't it? Considering the mess you have here, I wouldn't risk it.'

He snorted but left.

About fifteen minutes later, I heard footsteps. They sounded different. Not the quick shuffle policemen made when bored. These steps were confident, steady, each with its own rhythm.

First came the same policeman who had nearly put me into a coma with his glare earlier. Behind him walked someone else. A tall man in a suit, wearing it as if it were his second skin. Dark, polished, yet natural. The way people dressed when they had nothing to prove because they already knew everything.

His face was calm, not cold, but as if he felt nothing. He looked at me without surprise or curiosity. There was something in his eyes I couldn't understand. He didn't say anything. He simply took a piece of paper, signed it, and handed it back to the policeman. Nothing more.

Then he approached me, stopped a short distance away, and said, 'Come.'

Chapter Thirteen
The Truth

The door clicked shut behind me in such an ordinary way that it sounded as if I'd always belonged in that car, though I hadn't. Not even close. I wasn't sitting in the passenger seat. I was sitting in a minefield. Next to me sat a man, older and rigid, wearing a suit that had seen more of life than fashion.

His hair was grey and thinning, and his hands were strong, the kind with knuckles that had never learned how to forgive. I couldn't take my eyes off him, but he didn't register me, not even for a second. Not out of the corner of his eye. Not even by accident.

When he looked up, he stared hard at the road as though I wasn't even there, as though I was less than air. Not the invisible kind, but more like smoke, the kind that clogs your lungs and lingers even when you want it gone.

'Thank you for coming,' I said.

Nothing.

'I just… I'm glad that… well, that someone called you. That I'm not completely alone.'

He gripped the steering wheel so tightly that his knuckles turned white.

'Don't talk,' he said, flat and uninterested, like someone mowing a lawn without wanting to hear it cry.

Silence followed.

I stared out the window. London flickered by, though we didn't seem to be going anywhere at all.

'Mum used to talk about you,' I tried again. 'She said you were… a fair man.'

The steering wheel creaked again as he squeezed it, then he let go, and in that single gesture there was more contempt than a hundred words could carry.

'Your mum… was my daughter,' he said through gritted teeth. 'And then she wasn't.'

'I… I don't understand.'

He laughed, but only for a second. It was cold, sharp, and gone as quickly as it came.

'Yeah. That's you all over, isn't it? You don't understand. Not a thing. You go around collecting shadows, leaving silence and blood behind you.'

I froze, because this wasn't just disgust anymore. This was hate. Slow, sticky hate that had been simmering for years and had finally reached the point of no return.

'I… I don't collect anything. But soon I will, when my dad —' I tried to finish, but he cut me off.

'I hate you. I don't care who you are. You're not my grandson,' he said, calmly.

And that… that hit like a punch.

'But why? I haven't —'

'No, not you,' he interrupted. 'Your father. That bastard. The one who came and stole my daughter. Turned her into something that was never mine again.'

He pulled the steering wheel. The car jolted, but he didn't stop.

'She was meant to live. Have a normal life. A husband. A house. Maybe hate me, but at least be here. On this earth, and instead? She gave birth to you in a place I could no longer go, no longer see her, no longer hold her.'

I stared at him.

'But… Mum went willingly. To be with me. To look after…'

'She didn't want to! Did you know that? She didn't want to go with him. He took her. Took everything from her. You call that 'willing'?'

'I… I didn't know. She told me something else. So did my father.'

'Of course, because you're his. Just like him. You smile the same. Look the same. You know what? Forget it!'

He pulled up outside a house. Sudden. Turned the engine off, slicing through the noise like a knife.

Opened the door.

'Right. Out you get. And don't forget who you've got to thank for the silence at home.'

It was a house that smelled of tea and old carpets, of things you're not supposed to touch. A house that didn't follow modern trends or keep tidy, but still had something whole about it, as if no one had ever moved out and time had simply slowed down. When I stepped inside, I stood in the hallway for a moment, coat wet, boots dirty, while cold air clung to the ceiling, reluctant to move.

Grandad said nothing. He just closed the door behind me and walked off to the kitchen without looking back. Standing there, I felt it clearly. The anger was gone, the hate long passed. What remained was exhaustion, heavy and deep, rising not from life but from loss. I slowly stepped into the living room, which was full of books, mugs, and forgotten memories scattered around as if they'd never left.

On the shelf, I saw a photo and stopped.

It was Mum. Young, hair windswept, eyes wide open like the sky.

'That was in Cornwall,' Grandad said behind me.

I jumped. I hadn't heard him come in.

'She was eighteen. Hmm… had a new camera. Took that herself with the timer. Said she looked 'alive' that day, you know.'

He sat on the edge of an old armchair, his eyes fixed on her. Not on me.

'She looked beautiful,' I said.

'She was. Even though she hated it when people said so. She preferred it when someone called her clever or brave. That meant more to her.'

'Yeah… that's my mum, alright.'

We sat in silence for a moment, and then I took a seat across from him. Neither of us spoke, but the room felt a little warmer. Still unfamiliar, but not as cold.

'You never knew me,' Grandad said quietly.

'And I never knew you. But you know, today, when I saw you in that cell, I recognised you. In your face. In your eyes. And for a moment, I hated you, because I saw him in you. But now…' He shook his head. 'Now I see her.'

Tears rose to the edge of my eyes, the kind I wasn't expecting. Not the cinematic kind, just the quiet sort that sit there like your soul whispering, 'I know too.'

'I miss her,' I said.

Grandad nodded.

'So do I.'

He got up slowly, walked over to a cabinet, and began rifling through it gently, as if afraid to disturb the past too loudly. After a minute, he pulled out a small envelope and handed it to me carefully.

'She left this with me before she went. Wrote that if I ever saw you, I should give it to you.'

Taking it in my hand was the strongest moment of all. The paper was yellowed, the handwriting bold and sharp. I didn't read it straight away. I just held it, and something inside me began to settle.

'You hungry?' he asked, his voice suddenly more human.

'Yeah... a bit.'

'I'll make you something. You're not from Hell, are you. Of course you eat.'

I smiled, and the room smelled of tea and old memories.

We sat opposite each other at a small wooden table, the surface cracked in ways that would make modern designers weep. Next to us, a teapot, two plates, one scratched so much it looked like runes. Bread. Butter. A bit of cheese.

We ate in silence. No comments. Just... normal. And yet, still a bit strange.

'Do you have any family left?' I asked.

Grandad didn't look at me. He just shrugged.

'No... All gone.'

I turned the bite over in my mouth and said, 'I know some of them. Not all, but a few were in Heaven. I'll take you there one day, and to see Mum. When... you know, when...'

It was only after I said it that I realised how it sounded. Like we were planning a visit.

Grandad looked at me, eyes narrowing. Not harshly, more surprised. But then he nodded slowly.

'That'd be nice,' he said.

Silence again. Just the sound of tea being poured into a cup.

'And what about you?' he asked after a while. 'What are you doing here? With us?'

I looked up.

'I'm looking for my dad.'

He didn't respond. He just stared at me, everything slowing.

'He vanished. We don't know where he is. He didn't come back from the human world. So I went to find him.'

'And whose bloody idea was it to send you?' Grandad said through clenched teeth. The look wasn't curious. It was sharp.

'No one sent me,' I shrugged. 'I went on my own.'

Silence. Then he said, 'So you just got up and thought, 'I'll go find Death,' did you?'

'Well... actually Alan did. His servant. Assistant. He told me I should go.'

In that moment, Grandad froze. Not just his face. His whole body. He put his cup down slowly, then left the room without a word. I sat there for a moment, confused. Then I heard him coming back. When he returned, he was holding something in his arms. A small wooden box, older than the house itself. He placed it gently on the table and opened it.

Inside was a lump of black, misshapen stone. And when I looked closely, I realised its surface was moving ever so slightly, like it was breathing.

'This,' Grandad said quietly, 'was given to me by your father the day he took my daughter.'

He didn't say the day he married her or the day he loved her.

He said took.

'He said the stone was ancient. Magical. One of a kind. That it could summon Death and control him. Bind him. Take his power.'

I stared at the stone, eyes widening.

'That... that can't be real.'

'It is.'

My thoughts were racing.

'But if you have it, and he's gone, then someone must've caught him, right? Humans? But that makes no sense. If the stone's here and he's not, then what? Someone took him? Controlled him? But how? Where?'

Grandad didn't answer. He just looked at me, waiting for me to work it out. The stone pulsed faintly, like it had a heartbeat of its own. I could barely breathe. 'Wait,' I whispered, 'if the stone's here, then no one could've captured him. Because without it—'

'He can't be bound,' Grandad finished. Then he took a deep breath, pushed back his chair, and stood up. 'You're a foolish boy.'

I blinked.

'What?'

'Foolish,' he repeated. 'If humans had truly captured him, they'd need the stone. But they don't. It's here, with me. Which means only one thing. Death isn't in the human world.'

I stayed seated, and for the first time, let myself accept that none of this made sense.

'So where is he?' I asked.

'I don't know,' Grandad replied. 'But I do know what it means. That Alan sent you on your own. With no protection. No map. Nothing.'

I froze.

'He… he said he was sending me because he believed I could handle it.'

'And you believed him?' Grandad's eyes narrowed. 'Just like your father. Always trusting those who whisper in his ear.'

'Alan was his servant,' I said softly. 'He trusted him. He was always with us.'

Grandad shook his head.

'Servant's just a word, Tonny. You know what a servant does best? He listens. And then he serves whoever offers more.'

I swallowed.

'Do you know something about Alan I don't?'

Grandad sat back down, his body tired but his eyes still burning.

'I know he's human. But not an ordinary one. He knows about The Deep, about Heaven and Hell. He knew your father. Knew me. He was there when Death came for my daughter. And it was him who brought me that stone. Your father sent it through him, told me if anything ever happened, this was the key. To protect, but also to control.' He paused, then added more quietly, 'I never used it. I hoped your father would protect you himself. And that my daughter would be safe.'

'She was,' I whispered. 'In her own way.'

Grandad nodded. And for the first time, I saw something different in his eyes. Maybe peace.

'Your father wasn't a monster, Tonny. He was Death. He only ever did what he knew. But the world began to crack, and this,' he pointed to the stone, 'was never meant to see the light of day.'

My head lifted as the realisation hit me.

'Alan had the key,' I said suddenly. 'To the forbidden room. The one no one was allowed into. He said Dad gave it to him.'

Grandad's face froze even more.

'Then you have to go back. Immediately.'

'Wait… why?'

'Because this isn't just about your father. This is a betrayal. Something deeper than loss. If Alan went into that room, he knew exactly what to look for and why.'

My heart thudded.

'But Alan's just a servant.'

Grandad leaned in, his voice firm.

'And a servant, Tonny, can serve anyone.'

Chapter Fourteen
Back in the Deep

The thread snapped. Thin, black, soaked in shade. Martus froze as if someone had struck him in the heart, the one he had long since stopped showing to the world. The needles in place of hands trembled. One clattered onto the table, and another reluctantly withdrew into the folds of fabric drifting through the air like drowsy shadows.

He sat hunched at the table, his knee-high socks slipping down under the weight of gravity, and his beard brushing the crown seam of his patch-covered coat. Behind him, the sewing hoop rattled like it was having a fit. A ball of purple yarn rolled off the next table, muttered a curse, and tumbled into a dark corner. And he, the master of needles, the mage of fabric, the man with eyes like a stitched-up black moon, sat in silence and did not sew. Everything was different now. Ever since Tonny disappeared. 'Stupid little brat,' Martus muttered.

The needles twitched around his wrists, as if agreeing with him, though they didn't look convinced. Even they weren't sewing with certainty anymore. On the floor beneath the table lay Tonny's old cloak. The first one, the one with the stain from a lemon biscuit and the pocket that never held what it was meant to hide. Martus stared at it like a ghost he had never dared to send away.

In the fabric of reality the wind rose, not outside or in the room, and the ground trembled. Only slightly, but for someone who lived in the deep tunnels of The Deep, it felt like a slap across the senses. 'Him again,' Martus breathed.

Alan.

Since the day the world had changed, since the Council had been seated and Tonny had vanished, everything in The Deep had shifted. Alfonzo De Death, father of Death and grandfather to that restless boy in boxer shorts, had taken up the Mark of Power. And now, running the palace, was Alan. The same Alan who had served, bowed, polished Death's boots, and always acted like he didn't have a shadow of his own. The Alan who had stood just one step to the side, always watching.

He was giving orders now.

Martus didn't say it aloud, but the thought hung in the air like a speck of dust that refused to settle. Tonny was gone. No one had told him. Not officially. But the silence was too loud. No one had asked for a new suit. No one had ordered more invisible boxer shorts. And no one had come in whining that trousers weren't proper Council attire.

Martus sighed. The needles slipped back into their cases, and he sat down. At the threshold of the workshop, the seam lit up. That old symbol that always flared when someone entered without knocking. Now it burned. Slow and stubborn, like a fuse that couldn't be bothered to explode. Martus didn't even turn around.

He just said softly, 'If you've come for me, Alan... you'll have to unpick me first.'

The thread caught. Martus pulled the fabric closer to his eyes, though everything still looked blurry through his glasses. The needles in place of fingers trembled, not from cold, but from a strange pressure building inside him. The cloth was dark grey, tinged with shadows that never quite washed out. It was the kind of fabric that protected the soul, even when the soul didn't know it needed protecting. 'This is the last one,' he muttered to himself, though he didn't really believe it.

Stitch by stitch, slow and precise, quiet as a prayer. Around him, rolls of fabric hung like dead stories no one wanted to wear anymore. The old lamp on the table crackled, and in the corner, a ball of red yarn whispered to itself. When the shirt was finished, he straightened his back. The needles hissed softly as they withdrew, and Martus simply held the shirt in his hands for a moment. It was simple and perfect, like a promise never spoken aloud. 'The brat would crumple it anyway,' he growled, but his voice sounded hollow.

One step at a time, slow as though on ice, he entered the corridor after opening the workshop door. Tonny's room was at the end of the east wing, first floor. He knew it by heart, but when he got there, something had already changed. The lock was glowing red, and beside it stood Alan, with his hands behind his back, a smile that didn't reach his eyes, and the look of someone who had just learned what power tastes like.

'Where are you going, Martus?'

'To his room.'

'No point. It's sealed.'

'I just want to leave the shirt there.'

Alan reached out a hand slowly.

'Give it to me.'

Martus held on a second too long, then placed it in Alan's palm. Alan tossed it over his arm like a rag. 'I'd say you're sentimental, but that would be generous.'

Martus clenched his teeth. The needles scraped against themselves. 'One more thing,' Alan added as he turned to go. 'If I see you again in corridors where you don't belong, the Dustdreads will get a new target.'

As if carrying groceries, he walked away, calm and casual.

Martus stood there with empty hands and a full heart, and something inside him stitched its first knot. He stayed long after Alan turned the corner. Quietly, but his teeth were grinding like they were trying to finish a thought he couldn't say aloud. It was anger. The real kind. The kind that sits deep, quiet and wordless. The kind that doesn't burn the skin but smoulders beneath the ribs. The kind no needle or stitch could fix.

He returned to the workshop, but not to sew. Instead, he reached under the table for a box. It was old, cracked, fastened with three latches and a knot of black thread. He undid it in one pull. Inside lay a bundle of shadow-ribbons, a small dagger-pin, and a piece of cloth the colour of invisibility. It was magic for sewing what shouldn't be seen, and for one purpose only: to watch.

The punishment was brutal in Deep, where magic was forbidden — and Martus never used it. But this time was different. And he was ready to face the consequences. He stitched the pin into the inner sleeve of the shirt, the very one Alan had taken. The fabric was still warm. He knew Alan wouldn't take it straight to storage, and he was right. The edge of the shirt trembled. The thread carrying the binding spell stirred.

Martus closed his eyes, drove one needle into the table, and twisted the other slightly as if tuning an aerial. The image rippled. It wasn't sharp, but it was clear enough. Alan was in a corridor, heading towards the West Stairwell.

'Of course you are,' Martus muttered. 'Straight down, obviously.'

He pressed his palm to the cloth, found its pulse, and then slipped into it.

Silence, footsteps, darkness.

He followed Alan not from afar, but through the thread, through the fibre he had made. He was with him. He could feel his movement, his breath.

Alan stopped and looked around. Martus clenched his jaw and held the tension of the thread without moving. Half-grown into the wall where the prisoner stores had once been, the old hidden door yielded as Alan unlocked it. It was supposedly unused now, but he had the key.

He slipped inside. Martus disconnected from the thread and ran. He moved silently, with needles drawn in, precise. The door was open, just a narrow gap. The light inside barely reached the floor, and behind a pillar he hid. The air was still.

A voice spoke, low and measured. It wasn't Alan's. This one belonged to someone in control.

'Well done. You handled it admirably.'

Alan waited a second. He always waited.

'It was easy. He's thick. Literally jumped into the human world thinking he'd find his dad.'

'And instead,' the man said, 'he walks straight into his own fall.' Martus leaned forward, just enough to see the edge of the room. He couldn't make out the speaker's face. Just a figure. Tall. Still. Comfortable in the dark. 'In five days, he'll be human. Permanently. And Deep will lose its heir.'

Alan nodded.

'If he'd stayed, the power might've reached him. But out there, with no artefact and no guidance, he'll fade. Bit by bit. No name, no claim.' The man carried on. 'And we'll take what's left.'

The silence after that wasn't empty. It sat there like something alive. Martus felt something inside him pulling tight, then breaking. Not a feeling. A thread. Alan moved to a cabinet near the far wall, unlocked it, and opened it slowly. Martus froze. Alan took out a small box and handed it to the man. The man opened it.

Inside was a black, cracked crown, thin streams of smoke rising from it, steady and silent. Martus squinted. Then frowned. *Hold on. That crown. I know that crown. That's Alfonzo De Death's. I lined that thing myself. Years ago. Why the hell is Alan holding it?*

'You weren't seen?' the man asked.

'No, sir. Tonny saw movement, that's all. I disappeared before he could get close. Didn't see my face. I wore a cloak.'

The man nodded.

'Good... good. Then we've got everything we need. The plan's in place.'

Martus stayed where he was. Still breathing, but slower now. Careful. *That voice... I've heard it before. Not often. Not recently. But I've heard it. But where?*

He felt the start of something stir in his chest. Trying not to panic, he reminded himself that he wasn't afraid, only worried about Tonny. That boy. That mess in boots. The brat who once pulled up all his blue flowers thinking they were weeds. The kid who never asked permission but still showed up like he belonged. Who, somehow, did. And now he was in real danger.

Alan, who was quiet, polite and clean-fingered, had taken a step too far. And Martus knew, without saying it out loud: He wasn't going to let that pass.

Chapter Fifteen
Guidebook

Martus slammed the workshop door shut, though this time he didn't lock it. The needles around his wrists vibrated like a silent alarm, and the fabrics folded themselves back into their corners, as if even they knew this wasn't the time for stitching, but for action.

Three knocks landed on the pantry door, after he had slipped through a passageway smelling of glue, flowers, and baked sadness, after he had rushed down the corridor.

'If you're the one who keeps nicking my secret biscuits, I swear I'll—' Maria opened the door mid-threat. 'Martus?'

'We need to talk. Now! But shhh...'

He pulled her inside so fast she nearly dropped the tray of herbs in her hands.

'This is my kitchen, not your personal theatre stage, you sewing ghoul!'

'Shut it, or Alan will have you stitched to the ceiling and grind me into thread.'

Maria fell silent, which was, frankly, a first since before the revolution. Martus led her to the table, shoved aside a basket of biscuits, sat her down, and remained standing. The needles in his arms buzzed like angry bees.

'I found Tonny!'

Slowly Maria froze, like a clock stilled of its ticking yet twitching in its hands. 'What did you just say?'

'Alan sent him to the human world. He didn't tell anyone. He faked the order. If he had stayed in Deep, the power of Death would have found him. But out there, in the human world, after five days —'

'He becomes fully human,' Maria finished. 'And he'll never be able to inherit his father's power.'

'Exactly.'

Silence followed. It gripped the throat though no word was spoken. With a sharp motion Maria stood, and the table groaned beneath her.

'I'm going to kill that little weasel.'

'You can't,' Martus hissed. 'He's powerful, protected, with Dustdreads in his pockets. And he isn't working alone.'

'What do you mean, not alone? Who else?'

'I don't know. He was speaking to someone. I couldn't see their face, but whoever it was, they knew. They knew everything.'

Maria clenched her fists until her knuckles cracked.

'Tonny's like a son to me. When he was little, he used to draw skulls on my pie tins. But he never hurt anyone. And now he's out there on his own?'

'Yes,' Martus nodded. 'And if he stays, he'll lose everything… even his life.'

Maria breathed deeply, her eyes turning hard. Then she said, with utter seriousness, 'Then we're going.'

'What?'

'I'll take a biscuit pouch, you take your needles, and we're going to save the Prince of the Deep. I'm not leaving my boy in that awful world alone.'

Martus stared at her for a long moment, then shook his head slowly.

'It's not about who goes first. It's about the fact that we're going at all.'

'Right. And how, exactly?' Maria sat on a flour sack, which puffed quietly beneath her.

Martus didn't answer straight away. He stared into the distance as the needles curled into his palms like shy spider legs.

'Well... I know a place. An old entrance, from when Deepers could still slip in and out of Deep now and then. It's closed off, but not sealed.'

Maria narrowed her eyes.

'Wait... you mean that old shaft under the kitchen?'

'That's the one.'

'Martus, it's dark down there. Really dark. And I say that as someone who cooks in a windowless cellar.'

'Darkness never killed anyone.'

'No... but Deep has.'

There was a pause. Then Maria spoke quietly.

'Poor boy.'

Martus didn't move, but his voice softened.

'He won't make it alone. Maybe he's got a name. Maybe he's got blood. But he hasn't got knowledge. And more importantly, he hasn't got anyone.'

Maria stood, brushing flour off her apron, though it didn't help much.

'Alright then. Let's go. But...'

'But what?'

'What if people see us? You've got needles instead of hands and I look like I've escaped a bakery, not Hell.'

'That's exactly the point,' said Martus.

'We don't know anything about them. Only what's written. And those books... I mean... we need those books.'

'You mean, guidebooks?'

'Guidebooks,' Martus nodded.

'Back when Deep was still Deep, and not what it is now, there was a section in the library on the human world. How they speak. How they act. What offends them. What confuses them.'

Maria nodded slowly.

'Yellow-spined volumes, right? I used to dust them and swear they were watching me.'

'Those are the ones. Volumes forty-three to sixty-one. Access for external diplomats only. And rulers.'

'So... banned for us.'

'Exactly.'

Maria looked at him. Then at the door. Then back again.

'Fine. We're stealing knowledge.'

'Quietly. Alan's got guards everywhere. And the library's beneath the Council. Three floors down, five locked corridors, and one seal.'

'And you know how to break it?'

Martus narrowed his eyes. The needles gave a faint, metallic chime.

'No... but I'll find out.'

Maria smirked.

'Alright then, Needle-boy. You bring the tools, and I'll bring the biscuits. It's going to be a long night.'

*** *** ***

The corridors were quiet. Suspiciously quiet. Martus walked ahead, pressing a needle against the lock of a door that looked like a forgotten lift shaft. In reality, it was an old service passage leading straight to the left wing of the library.

'Don't talk. Breathe through your nose,' he muttered over his shoulder.

Maria huffed behind him, clutching her biscuit pouch and wearing a thoroughly unimpressed expression.

'I do breathe through my nose. You breathe less. You're poking holes in the air.'

'Very funny. Now shush.'

A metallic click followed. The door creaked open, and they stopped. Inside, it was dark and damp. No one had turned on the lighting. Not because it was broken, but because Alan had sealed access for anyone not on his list. And Martus most definitely wasn't.

'Guidebooks. *Interdimensional Contact*, Series Forty to Sixty. We're after Volume Forty-Two. You know your numbers?'

'Of course. I'm a cook, not a moron.'

'We'll see.'

They slipped inside.

The library in Deep wasn't quiet, at least... not in the way you might expect. The books whispered. Literally. Each one held living information, and sometimes it wanted to talk. Some shelves murmured. One spat out dust whenever someone got too close.

Maria reached for a book, and it hissed at her.

'Right. That one can stay there.'

Martus, meanwhile, was climbing a built-in stairway, needles tapping the spines with practised precision.

Then they heard footsteps that were rhythmic and heavy, not human. Maria froze as Martus snuffed out the lamp. At the entrance stood a guard clad in black armour, a spear in hand. Its gaze was empty, with cracks where the eyes should have been. There was no emotion.

After a quick glance around, Martus reached into his pocket and threw a biscuit. It landed in the corner with a soft plunk. The guard turned and walked toward the sound. Not hesitating, but moving like a machine.

The footsteps faded.

Maria let out a breath.

'That wasn't the plan, was it?'

'It was. Improvised. And delicious.'

'You got it?'

'Yes. Forty-Two. And a few extras, just in case.'

'Then let's move.'

They crept back the way they came, just as slowly. When they had shut the service door behind them, Maria finally spoke.

'Tonny's lucky to have us.'

Martus nodded firmly.

'And we've got some reading for a long night,' said Martus.

The greenhouse in Deep was old and forgotten, locked with two bolts and marked by a helpful little sign that read *Definitely Do Not Enter*.

'This is it?' Maria whispered, as if she was afraid the moss might hear her.

'Yes,' Martus grunted. 'Official expedition point. Back in the day, we used it to send out photosynthesis. Now we're sending ourselves.'

'Sounds safe.'

'It's not.'

Martus leaned into the door, and it creaked so loudly that Maria jumped. Beyond it, the greenhouse opened up, damp and steamy, and it reeked of mushrooms that looked as if they were plotting a murder.

'Wow...' Maria clutched a biscuit to her chest. 'This is worse than your socks.'

'Really? You still remember Needle Season of seventy-four?'

'The whole Deep remembers Needle Season of seventy-four, Martus.'

'Good!'

Inside, there was a low hum. It was not mechanical, but more like something quietly furious. At the far end stood a huge, organic-looking tube. It appeared alive, wrapped in roots, with lights flickering along its sides in a way so miserable it was almost poetic.

'So… what now?' Maria asked.

Martus pulled out an old scrap of paper and a seed.

'This will get us through. The Archivist gave it to me in exchange for a bit of stitching, and because I once saved his leg. Or his head. I can't remember which bit he had extra.'

Maria took a step back, then another.

'So we're going to get absorbed by a plant?'

'Not exactly. It will break us down into particles that light can carry, and then beam us into the human world.'

'And we'll reassemble on the other side?'

'Hopefully.'

Maria drew in a long breath and tightened her grip on the biscuit pouch.

'Alright... but I'm bringing these. If I'm going to look like some convict crawling out of a black hole, I at least want something sweet.'

Martus gave a small nod.

'And the humans... are you not afraid?' she whispered. 'You've got needles for hands. I sound like a fire alarm. They'll notice us at once.'

'Again, Maria?' Martus sighed. 'Then we run. Or we stand still and pretend we're part of an art installation. Either way, keep your mouth shut.'

She frowned. 'That is not very reassuring. I meant... more like...' Her words faltered.

Martus looked at her, patient but sharp. 'You mean the spoons in your body?'

Maria lowered her head and nodded.

'Right. No one is going to be upset by our spoons,' he said briskly. 'So here. Quickly. Drink this.' He drew a small vial from his pocket and pressed it into her hand.

'What is it?' she asked.

'It will make you... a little more human. Only for a couple of hours.'

Maria stared at him, eyes softening. 'Thank you, Martus. But... why not drink it yourself?'

He shook his head. 'I have tried. Many times. It does not work on me.'

Maria lifted the vial and drank. Almost at once her skin smoothed, the sharp edges gone. No spoons, no strange shapes pressing out. She touched her arms, smiling in wonder.

'Come on. No time for this now,' Martus said. His voice was firm. 'And do not get used to it. Soon you will be back to normal.'

'Nothing ever is. But we're still going.'

Martus placed the seed into the centre of the tube. It began to pulse faintly, like something waking up that probably should have stayed asleep.

Maria shivered.

'This burns. Is that normal?'

'It's the Deep.' They looked at each other for a moment. Just that. 'Right then. Let's go save a boy who is completely unprepared for it,' said Martus.

'And destroy Alan.'

'That's a bonus.'

They stepped in.

The light swallowed them, and the tube closed its mouth. At first, there was nothing. Just silence. The kind that echoed inside the skull like the haunting consequence of a choice already made.

Then came a sudden snap. Maria let out a cry, not from pain but from sheer shock. Their bodies broke apart into threads of light. It felt like dissolving into dust, scattered through a beam, and then swept away.

They flew through darkness, through layered dimensions that smelled faintly of burnt sugar and aged embroidery. A wooden spoon, needles, clothing, hair, and skin came back as their forms reassembled in a single flash. And suddenly, there were paving stones beneath them. Wet, glistening, and unmistakably part of the human world.

Maria landed hard, seated squarely in a ventilation space between two rubbish bins. Martus remained standing, while the needles around his wrists still trembled as if trying to understand what had just occurred. Maria straightened herself, dusted off her backside, and took a deep breath.

She immediately started coughing.

'Oh Deep, the air here smells like a dustbin.'

Martus inhaled slowly.

'London. Judging by the stench, that would be accurate.'

Glancing around, Maria tried to judge the time. Evening or morning, it was hard to know. There was no welcome, no glow at the end of the journey. Only reality, set against a city humming with life, sirens, shouting, laughter, and the rumble of traffic.

She sat down slowly on the edge of the kerb.

'That was the worst method of transport I have ever used.'

'It was the only one available,' Martus replied as he looked around. 'Right then. We are here. Now we need to find Tonny before he becomes entirely human.'

Maria stood up again, picked up her pouch of biscuits, and strode onto the street with firm steps.

'I hope he has at least tasted something decent by now. Because if he is starving, I will slap him myself.'

Martus rustled his coat, tucked the pendant with the guidebook deeper into his pocket, and sighed as he followed behind her.

'This is going to be a very long day.'

Chapter Sixteen
The Stone

'So you're saying it was Alan?'

It was as if he brushed the back of history when his fingers traced the spines of the volumes, leaning on an old oak stool as he reached for the shelf.

'Strange. He always came across as the sort who waters plants rather than weaves schemes.'

'I thought the same,' I said quietly. 'But now it all fits. He knew that if I stayed in the Deep, my power would eventually awaken. But if I stayed here...'

'In five days, you'll become fully human,' Grandad finished, his voice sharp. 'After that, there's no way back. No inheritance. No gates.'

I nodded. Hearing it hurt. It was as though something inside me had already begun to close. Meanwhile, Grandad pulled a book from the bottom shelf. It creaked softly as he lifted it.

'I wrote this,' he said. 'It's old. And honest. I was fascinated by your father. Not as Death. As a being. As a force that shaped the laws of the world.'

He opened the book. The pages were handwritten, filled with notes along the margins and illustrations that felt almost alive.

'Here,' he said, pointing. 'This part is about the stone. The one he gave me when he took my daughter. He told me that if the world ever began to fall apart and he disappeared, this would be the only thing capable of turning the tide. Of opening the way. Of summoning... balance.'

Shadows shimmered where they had no right, across a matte black stone he placed between us. I stared at it and felt something tighten in my chest.

'Do you think it could open the way back?' I asked.

'Perhaps, but using it is no simple matter. It's not a key, Tonny. It's a gate... and every gate takes something in return.'

At that moment, something changed. Grandad lifted his head. And I... I felt it before I saw her.

Movement. Outside the window. We both turned.

Behind the old, dust-streaked glass stood a girl, perfectly still, calm, as though she had always been there. Her hair fell over her shoulders, and her eyes were dark and focused.

'That's...' I whispered.

'Do you know her?' Grandad mumbled.

'No... but I think she knows me.'

I didn't know why she was here. Or how she had found me. But I didn't feel any threat. Only something I couldn't quite name.

'Let her in,' Grandad grumbled. 'But if this is a trap, I swear I'll write a will just so I can leave you out of it.'

I opened the door. Lucy stood quietly, as if she had been waiting. There was no smile, only the faint tilt of a head to one side.

'Good evening,' she said. Her voice was soft and unhurried, but every word landed exactly where it was meant to.

Without a moment's pause she entered, looking around, once I had stepped aside. Not with awe. More like someone confirming what they already suspected.

'This is Lucy,' I said, although there was no need.

Grandad nodded silently. He watched her, and she watched him just as intently. A hush settled over the room. And suddenly, I had the strange feeling that this silence did not belong to us.

'Sorry,' she added. 'I didn't mean to spy. But... I knew you were here.'

'How do you know that?'

There was a pause, as if she was deciding what she could say. What she should say.

'I don't know. I just... feel it. Like when a storm is getting closer.'

It was strange, but not threatening. Not frightening either. It felt more like hearing a song that reminds you of something, even though you have no idea what it is.

With a slightly nervous smile, I shook my head.

'Look, if you're following me, just say so. I've seen worse things than that today anyway.'

Lucy smiled faintly, but she didn't answer. Just then footsteps echoed from the hallway, and Grandad appeared in the doorway with a tin of biscuits in one hand and a napkin in the other.

'I just... biscuits,' he muttered, setting them on the table like he'd caught us in something but wasn't going to ask.

He gave Lucy a long look. He didn't say a word, but his eyebrows shifted in that unmistakable way that said: Yes, I see there's a girl here. And yes, I know you have absolutely no idea what to do about it. Then he vanished again and left us there.

Lucy sat down carefully. For a moment, she just stared at the tin as though she was afraid to take one. I nudged it closer to her.

'They're fine. A bit hard, but still good. That's the style around here.'

She broke off a piece and looked at me with a different gaze. Not like a boy from the street. But like someone she knew. Or maybe someone she should have known. And I felt that shiver again. But this time, it was something else entirely. Grandad returned with the book. It was heavy and black, with a silver symbol embossed along its spine. He handed it to me, though his eyes remained fixed on Lucy.

He had noticed there was still something she was holding back. And it was clear he wanted to know what it was.

'This is about him,' he said quietly. 'Everything I ever discovered. Even the things I would have preferred not to know.'

I placed the book on the table, but I didn't look at it.

I looked at Lucy.

'The stone...' I began. 'Grandad says it might open a gate. Help me get back to the Deep.'

Lucy said nothing. She played with a piece of napkin between her fingers, then slowly shook her head.

'That stone won't take you home.'

Silence filled the room.

'What do you mean?'

'It holds power, yes. I can feel it. But... it isn't yours. It doesn't answer to you. Because...' She looked straight into my eyes. 'The power is already inside you, Tonny.'

My heart skipped a beat. Then another. Grandad pulled up a chair and sat down slowly, as if he needed to be closer, but not interfere.

'What do you mean?' I whispered.

Lucy straightened. For the first time since she arrived, she looked completely calm. It was as though she had made a decision — that she had to say it now, all of it.

'One week ago... I was supposed to die.'

She said it without hesitation. As a fact. Not for drama.

'I was standing at a bus stop. It was raining. The night was dark. I knew it was the end. I could feel it. Death came.'

Grandad didn't move.

I didn't think I was breathing.

'I saw him. He looked... tired. Broken. Like someone carrying the entire weight of the world and knowing he couldn't hold it any longer. Still, he walked towards me. Slowly. Without a word.' She closed her eyes, as if reliving the moment. 'When he stood in front of me, he looked at me... but he didn't see me. As though he was searching for something else. Or someone.'

She opened her eyes again. 'Then his knees gave out. He collapsed. I caught him as best I could. And in that moment... he placed a hand on my shoulder.' She swallowed. 'And he said, 'This power I give to you. For my son. Keep it safe. When the time comes... you will know him.''

She fell silent.

So did I.

Grandad stared at her, rigid and quiet, watching her face.

'And then he disappeared. As if silence itself had taken him.'

For a while, no one spoke.

The old clock's ticking in the corner seemed mocking.

'So...' I began, but stopped myself.

Lucy nodded.

'The power you're looking for, the one you expected from your father, is in me now. And I found you because I was meant to.'

Grandad breathed deeply and leaned back in the chair. 'Well, I'll be...' he whispered.

I didn't know whether to be afraid, to cry, or to laugh. Before I even had a chance to say anything — whether it was 'What?', or 'What do you mean it's inside me?', or even 'Look, I only came for tea and answers, not a bloody destiny' — something happened.

A sharp sound came, like wind on stone. Grandad stood up. Faster than I would ever have expected. Lucy turned towards the door, but I was looking at the window. Across the street, a woman stood completely still. Calm. Simply there. And then, without warning or cause, she dropped to her knees.

The children at the playground stopped. Even those who had been running. Even the one eating an ice cream. All of them turned to look in the same direction. The dust was not just dust.

It moved. It had shape, but no form. It was invisible, yet I recognised them.

Dustdreads.

'No,' I breathed.

'You can see them?' Lucy turned to me. Her eyes were wide, though not afraid.

She seemed perfectly aware and present.

'Yes,' I whispered. 'They're here. They're searching for—'

'The one who carries the power of Death,' she finished softly.

Grandad did not ask a single question. He was already pulling down the blinds and turning off the lights. He moved automatically, like someone who had always known when the unseen begins to look back.

Outside, there was a scream. Then another. And then came the most terrifying kind of silence. The kind where everyone is still alive, but no one is certain of it. We stood together in the dark. Three people and a stone on the table. And none of us knew how much time we had left.

Chapter Seventeen
Do Not Provoke

The pavement was harder than they had expected. People streamed past them like a herd that knew exactly where it was going, but had no patience for anyone who hesitated. Martus came to a stop at the traffic light and stared up at the flashing figure.

Green. Then red. Then green again.

Maria stepped up beside him, her brow furrowed with suspicion.

'Is this some sort of ritual?' she whispered.

Martus didn't answer right away. Instead, he reached inside his coat and pulled out the guidebook. It was a heavy volume, bound in worn cloth that smelled faintly of old ink and baked earth. An hour earlier he had marked the tab, and that was where he opened it. The needles slipped from his sleeves and flicked through the pages with the precision of a Swiss scissor-wielding assassin.

'Chapter Three,' he muttered. 'I quote: 'Crossing protocol. Follow the little man. If he is red, stay. If he is green, walk. If he is blinking, wait. If he starts dancing, run.''

He snapped the book shut with a dry sigh. 'So we wait for the green man. And if he starts doing a tap routine, we run.'

Maria scanned the street around them.

'And what if he never shows up?'

'Then we starve to death on the corner.'

The green man lit up. The crowd moved as one, sweeping forward like a tide. Martus and Maria hesitated for just a moment, then stepped in line and followed. As they crossed, Martus glanced over his shoulder at the light behind them. The city pulsed around him, strange and sharp in all the ways he hadn't expected.

'I'm impressed,' he muttered. 'But I hate that I trust it more than I trust Alan.'

They reached the far pavement and paused. The world continued to rush by in streams of noise and direction. People did not stop. They did not wander, only moved, and that unsettled Martus.

He turned to the first person he saw. It was an older man with a hat and a folded newspaper tucked under his arm.

'We're looking for... the Prince of Deep.'

The man stared at him for a second, then stepped carefully back.

'Right. Yeah. Mental health services are closed, mate. Try the police station. Might have someone there who'll chat to you.'

Martus nodded, entirely serious. Then turned to Maria.

'Police station. Sounds important.'

With a shrug, Maria adjusted her biscuit pouch.

'Sounds like somewhere people go when they've got problems.'

Martus reopened the guidebook. The needles buzzed faintly, alert and ready.

'Page twenty-four... here we go. Police: human authority entity. Identifiers include uniform, loudness, and a fondness for coffee. Do not provoke. Speak clearly. Do not say you are from the Deep.' He closed the book and slipped it back inside his coat. 'Well. That is reassuring. Anyway... we shall go.'

A gust slid through the crowd, casual as you like, dragging behind it the scent of petrol, chips, and something stranger, like wet concrete had just remembered it used to be a church. No one blinked. This was normal.

The city churned on, confident in its routine. Systems humming, signals flashing, people moving like they knew what was coming next. They didn't. They were still working it out, one blinking light at a time. Each one a test. None of them multiple choice.

As they headed in the direction the man had pointed, a boy passed them, laughing and glued to his phone. He stopped, glanced at Martus's hands, and stared. The tips of the needles were just visible beneath his sleeves.

'Whoa! That's sick! Where'd you get those? Amazon?'

Martus froze and turned slowly.

'On what?'

Maria quickly clutched the guidebook to her chest.

'That must be another human leader. Like the traffic light.'

Martus frowned.

'I hope this one doesn't flash.'

And then they gave him a look like he'd nicked the last biscuit and carried on. The man turned, smirking. 'Don't mind that lot. Come on,' said Martus.

The street split ahead.

To the left was a flashing sign marked POLICE. To the right... something far more interesting. Something fragrant. Maria stopped abruptly, as though she had caught a scent on the wind.

'Wait,' she whispered. 'Do you smell that? Butter. Sugar. Cinnamon. That's... that's magic.'

Martus sighed and lifted his nose as well.

'That's warm, sugary death.'

Maria didn't move. She was staring through the shop window.

'Cakes, Martus. They're selling cakes on actual shelves, like bread.'

'It is bread. For pampered tongues.'

Maria had already pushed open the door. A small bell chimed overhead, and warmth flooded over them, carrying the scent of caramel and pastries like an embrace.

Martus lingered in the doorway.

'Five minutes,' he muttered to himself. 'Ten, at most, and I am not eating anything.'

Inside, the shop was like a dream wiped clean with lemon glaze. Shelves were lined with cupcakes, croissants, and cakes in at least fifteen different styles — each arranged like a museum exhibit.

She pressed her nose gently to the glass of the display after drifting toward it, entranced.

'I could do this,' she whispered. 'Maybe even better.'

'Your biscuits can wake the dead,' Martus replied, 'which is slightly problematic here.'

'Shush! You!'

Behind the counter stood a young woman with bright blue hair and a lip piercing. Next to her stood a young man. He was smiling, all charming, with a messy bun and eyes that immediately gave Maria a once-over.

'Hi there,' he said.

'Fancy something sweet, or are you just admiring?' He leaned forward slightly and tilted his head. 'You've got the look of someone who knows what good dough feels like.'

Maria flushed.

'I... well... I bake. Quite a lot. I mean... professionally. Sort of.'

'I believe it. You've got baker's hands.'

He stepped in a little closer and winked. Martus moved in quietly behind her. His needles gave a faint metallic ting, a polite yet pointed reminder of their presence.

'Oi, Romeo. This isn't a casting call!' His tone was dry. His smile was not friendly.

Romeo raised his hands.

'Alright, mate. Chill. It was just a compliment.'

Martus didn't blink. The needles gave another soft click.

'Sure. But next time, keep your compliments away from her dough.'

Maria stared at him, mouth slightly open. 'Martus… did you just defend me?'

'No. I am simply protecting the future of Deep. Your biscuits are strategic assets.'

Romeo chuckled, reaching behind the counter.

'You two are weird. But entertaining. Here… that's on the house.' He slipped a small cake into a paper bag and handed it to Maria.

She lit up.

'Thank you! We'll… um… return the favour somehow. Maybe.'

Martus gave a curt nod. The needles clicked once more. Outside on the pavement, Maria held the little paper bag with the mini cake tucked inside.

'So… my biscuits are strategic, are they?'

'In The Deep, they are.'

'Right.'

They walked in silence for a while. Then Maria added, 'If you ever want more compliments, you could earn them. With, say, breakfast.'

Martus waved a hand like he was brushing off a fly but his eyes twitched, just enough to betray the calm. Up ahead, the building loomed, all concrete corners and bureaucratic charm, stinking faintly of stale power and old printers.

Muttering under his breath, Martus pulled out the guidebook after stopping: 'Police station. Place where human wrongdoings, misdeeds, and assorted unpleasantness are handled. Entry permitted only in cases of desperation, crime, or missing cats.'

Maria leaned over his shoulder.

'What kind of nonsense is that? Who wrote this? Lunatic?'

'Someone from our side. So… yes.'

They stood on the pavement, uncertain for a moment. Across the road, a man in a dressing gown came sprinting out of a house, waving a frying pan above his head and shouting,

'Someone shoot me! Please!'

Behind him, his wife stormed after him, wielding a carton of eggs.

'Mark! That's the twentieth time today! You didn't even finish your beer!'

On a bench nearby, a woman sat with complete serenity, holding a cardboard sign that read: *I was supposed to die today. Body disagreed.*

A bus rolled straight over a pedestrian. The person sat up a moment later, visibly annoyed, and began picking bits of tarmac out of their trousers.

Maria blinked and stared.

'Is this... is this what happens when Death... isn't?'

Martus nodded.

'No, Maria. This is normal. Humans are... well. Fragile, and slightly mad.'

Suddenly, an alarm blared. A police officer burst out of the station, waving a megaphone.

'No group drownings! If you want to jump off the bridge, registration is across the street at Milly's Café!'

Maria turned her head slowly toward Martus.

'And we're actually going in there?'

Martus nodded.

'Yes. But stay close. Around here, you might become a famous pastry faster than you can say 'flour.''

Maria looked at him. Just looked. With that particular expression of hers, the one that always hovered somewhere between 'I'm going to kill you' and 'I'll make you tea, you look dreadful.' Then she smiled. A real smile. It was beautiful.

'Alright, General,' she said softly. 'But if anyone bites me, I'm going back to Deep and setting fire to everything.'

Martus rolled his eyes, but as the station doors creaked open and another scream rose from the crowd, he pulled her just a little closer.

Enough to cover her back. Nothing too obvious. Maria leaned in ever so slightly. Then gave a small, theatrical shiver.

'Brrr... I'm actually scared. So... human. So draughty.'

Martus did not flinch. But the grip around her shoulders tightened a fraction.

'Don't worry,' he muttered. 'If anyone hurts you, I'll turn them into a tablecloth.'

Maria grinned. 'A red one?'

'Theirs.'

And together, they stepped inside.

Chapter Eighteen
I Can Handle It

The stone sat on the table like it knew more than it was letting on. Dark, heavy, and oddly patient, as if waiting for someone to say something foolish. It didn't pulse or glow or do anything cinematic. It just *was*, in that quietly threatening way only certain objects and retired teachers can manage.

Lucy had slipped into the next room, said she needed a moment to clear her head. I didn't argue. She looked pale in that honest way people do when they realise they've gone further than they meant to. So I stayed behind. Just me, Grandad, and the rock that may or may not have been older than sunlight.

'Do you think it'll work?' I asked, immediately regretting how hopeful I sounded.

Grandad didn't answer at first. He leaned on one elbow, eyes fixed on the stone like it might flinch. He had that faraway look, the one he used to get in traffic jams or during long sermons. Thoughtful, but slightly annoyed to be there.

I reached out. My hand hovered above the surface. Only the faint sense of thickened air lingered near it; no heat, no static, no sudden surge of destiny. Or maybe that was my imagination.

Grandad looked at me calmly, offering no false comfort, only the truth that this was real. The stone remained, dark, heavy, alive with presence.

Outside the silence held, not empty but paused, and Lucy hadn't come back. I was still there with Grandad, and with whatever that thing was, the thing pretending to be a stone. 'What if it doesn't work?' I asked again, the uncertainty catching in my throat.

'Then at least you'll know you tried.'

The stone felt like breath. I closed my eyes and whispered one word. 'Dad…'

As though something inside had begun to stir, the stone's surface twisted gently after first flickering into motion.

And then came a sound, it was more like a soft crack forming along one side, so fine it was barely visible. From that fracture, a thin wisp of smoke drifted upwards. And with it came something more.

It was not a clear image, not even a reflection, but a presence. A shape began to take form, only the outline of a large, weighted figure moving through shadow as though it had been walking for years. Darkness shrouded it, though not completely. What I saw was not dead; it looked tired, tired in a way that reached deep into the bones, like someone who had slept too long and was never meant to wake.

'Dad?' I whispered again.

The figure stopped. It didn't turn. It simply froze. And then, just as quickly as it had appeared, the image faded. The stone shuddered once beneath my hand, then grew still. Its glow vanished: the faint motion on its surface slowed and returned to that quiet, rhythmic breathing.

I sat there, motionless, my breath shallow and quick. My chest rose and fell too fast, like I'd been running. But I hadn't moved at all.

'Did you see that?' The words came out thin and brittle. I wasn't even sure I wanted the answer. Instead, he reached out and touched the stone, then pulled his hand back with a sharp breath, as if it had burned him.

'I saw it,' he said quietly, shaking his head.

'I don't know... but it was someone. Or something. And it looked like it heard you.'

Unsure of what I was agreeing to, I nodded. Something inside me was shifting, like a stone dropped into water too deep to see the bottom.

'I just don't understand...' I began, but couldn't find the end of the sentence.

Grandad finished it for me.

'Why didn't he stay? Why didn't he turn around?'

Silence settled between us, heavier than the stone. Then he said something that twisted in my gut like a knife turned slowly.

'Maybe he couldn't. Maybe he's not fully gone, but not truly here either. Maybe something is holding him... in between. And that stone... woke him up. Just for a second.'

Swallowing hard, I looked at the stone lying motionless, though I did not believe it was asleep. It was not a dream or my imagination. I had seen him. Or at least... something that had once been him.

'So he's alive,' I said, almost to myself.

'Maybe,' Grandad answered. 'But if he is, he's not in the human world.'

I looked down at the stone once more. I knew something with absolute certainty. My father was alive, but someone was keeping him asleep, and whoever was is doesn't want him waking up. I clenched my fists slowly. I have to find him, whatever it takes.

At that moment, Lucy appeared in the doorway. She didn't say anything at first. But something in her expression had shifted. Her shoulders locked before the stone registered. Narrowing eyes shifted slowly toward me.

'You felt him, didn't you?' she asked.

I just nodded. I couldn't speak. Lucy stepped closer to the table, like someone who already knew exactly what she would find. She placed her fingertips on the stone, and it responded. Again, it trembled. The motion was soft, almost like breath rising and falling in sleep. But this time, nothing more happened. Grandad stood, watching. He looked quiet, stern, but not unkind.

'He's in Deep,' Lucy said gently. 'I can feel it. His power is still there, pulsing. But it's bound, far beneath, and this stone cannot pull him out on its own.'

She straight through me, down to the parts I did not know how to name.

'You have to go,' she said, closing her eyes, placed both hands over her chest and took in a deep, slow breath. 'Maybe the power inside me. Maybe I can wake it. But...'

'But what?' I asked.

'It's not mine. It belongs to you. I'm just the carrier. So if you want to use it, you'll have to take it back.'

There was silence.

'How?' I asked. 'Physically? Mentally?'

She gave a slight smile. 'Honestly? I have no idea. But one thing is certain. I cannot give it to you. You have to take it. And only if you are ready.'

Grandad spoke then, his voice calm but firm.

'Are you, lad?'

Looking first at the stone and then at Lucy, I understood. Whatever happened next, there would be no way back. I stood before her, the stone quiet on the table, my head aching with doubt. Lucy raised her hands, her eyes fierce on mine.

'Are you sure I can handle it?' I asked quietly, though in truth, I did not really want to hear the answer.

'No,' she said without hesitation. 'But you're his son, and the power will try to match you. Or at least try.'

That wasn't exactly comforting. I took a breath and nodded. Her hands touched my chest, and the world vanished. Only pressure remained after everything shifted, within and without, taking light, sound, room, and Grandad with it. It was vast and brutal, as if a galaxy had wrapped itself around my ribs and was crushing inward to see how much I could bear before I broke.

It felt like someone was trying to pour an entire ocean into my chest. No, worse than that. It was darker, heavier, more ancient than any sea.

And it hurt. Oh Deep, it hurt.

Something stirred inside me. It wasn't pain and it wasn't a memory. More like pressure, coming from nowhere, giving no warning and asking no permission. Suddenly it felt like something was trying to turn me inside out. My whole body resisted, as if I was carrying something that had never truly belonged to me.

The force was sharp and hungry. It rose through my chest and into my throat. It wanted out. It wanted everything. And for a moment, I honestly didn't know whether to fight it or let it happen.

Then something shifted.

It came from deep within, from a place I had never really been aware of until now. Instead of fighting or noise there was only a quiet steadiness, firm without resistance. It carried no voice, no thought, only the feeling of something ancient and immovable settling in the centre of me. That was what brought it to a halt.

It was over.

My knees gave out. I hit the ground before I could make sense of what had happened. My hands were shaking. I felt empty and drained, like my body had just outrun something I hadn't even seen. Before I collapsed, Grandad caught me. Lucy still stood upright, but barely. She was pale, soaked in sweat, and breathing like someone who had just escaped drowning.

'It didn't work,' she said, before I could even ask.

I looked at her, my chest still rising and falling too fast.

'Why? Isn't the power mine?'

She gently shook her head.

'The power was given to me. By your father. But it is fractured, incomplete, passed on to someone who was never meant to carry it this long. I'm only a vessel, a step between. And without him here, it couldn't find the proper link. It's like having the key, but the lock is rusted shut.'

The floor held me still, my chest racing, my skull fevered, and what should have been transformation broke down into nothing but the hurt of a failed attempt.

A crack that nearly split me apart. And Lucy too.

Yet, there had been something. I was sure of it. Only for a moment, but it was there. Gone now, whatever it was, the flicker I felt when I touched her, a shift that might have come from me or from him.

And I'm still here, trying to catch my breath. Drained in a way that sleep won't fix. Not broken, but not quite whole either. Grandad cleared his throat, quiet, careful, like someone returning after something sacred has passed.

'Right then, moving forward,' he said. 'So how do you two plan on getting back? To Deep? If the stone doesn't work…'

'Roddy,' I said under my breath. More to myself than them, but they both heard it.

Grandad raised an eyebrow. 'What is a Roddy?'

'An artefact,' I said. 'Well… a friend. Okay, a puppet. A weird one, but he's always been with me. My dad made him. No one else can activate him, just me.'

Her head shifted to the side, the motion slight, her gaze steady. 'How do we find him?'

I closed my eyes. Somewhere distant, at the very edge of everything, I could feel it. A faint sensation at the back of my neck. Like someone calling me from very far away.

'Well… weird,' I said softly. 'I feel him. He's far but not gone.'

Grandad let out a long sigh and stood. Without another word, he went to the kitchen counter and began packing biscuits into a paper bag.

'Well then go,' he muttered. 'Find your little puppet. And while you're at it... save the world, would you?'

I looked at him.

His face had changed. Whatever anger had been there before was gone. No bitterness either, just something quieter now. Harder to place. It might have been pride, or close to it. Or maybe it was the echo of someone he'd lost, someone he couldn't quite bring himself to name.

I stood. Lucy stepped beside me. She placed her hand on my arm without saying a word. It was firm, stayed only a moment, then let go. It said: I'm here. I will go with you.

The stone was pressed into my hand only after a pause, once Grandad had given us the bag.

'Do not leave it here,' he said. 'You never know when you might need it again.'

With a nod, I moved with the others to the door. Lucy stood just outside, waiting, and I turned back once more before crossing the threshold.

'Oh, one more thing,' I added.

Grandad raised an eyebrow.

'Dustdreads. You know, those monsters. If they sense fear, they come for you, like sharks with blood.'

He gave me a long look. 'Go on.'

'So if you see them... vomit.'

'What?'

'Seriously. They love it. They go wild for it. One whiff and they'll dive for it like it's the best thing they've ever tasted. It's disgusting., but it works. If you're scared, just throw up. They'll be too busy eating it to bother with you.'

Grandad rolled his eyes. 'Go on, before I actually test it out just to get you out of my house.'

'Take care, Grandad.'

Into the cold air we stepped, and Lucy closed the door behind us with a hush like breath. And all I could do now was hope he had something in his stomach.

Chapter Nineteen
He's a Bit Odd, Charismatic

The door opened with a quiet squeak, as if it were hesitating to let two such beings inside. Martus stepped in first, with caution, like someone entering a sanctuary where, instead of statues, there were coffee vending machines. Maria followed right behind him, looking around as though she expected someone to leap out at any moment and start shouting at her in Latin.

'This is like… a waiting room in hell, only without the fire,' she muttered.

'I didn't know you'd been in hell.'

'Yes. I was… visiting someone. I mean… A long time ago.'

'Hmmm… I see.'

Martus walked over to a wall where a poster hung that read, 'TALK TO US – WE'RE HERE FOR YOU!' accompanied by a picture of a man smiling far more than should be humanly allowed.

'This looks like a threat,' he remarked, brushing the poster with a needle-finger. 'Or irony.'

A man in uniform passed by. He looked at them. Then looked again. And then a third time. Then thought better of it and kept walking.

Maria sat down on a plastic chair, which immediately creaked as if someone had just revealed a family secret to it.

'What now?' she asked.

'I don't know. Maybe… something like a human ritual. You queue up. Say something like, 'Hello, I'm looking for a prince'.'

'That sounds like a trap.'

'Then… 'Hello human, we are missing our royal ward'?'

'Worse.'

''We suspect your system has detained our heir to power and we require his location coordinates'?'

Maria looked at him.

'Martus. Give me a biscuit. Now.'

He automatically handed her one.

A few metres away, someone shouted, 'So what, I was supposed to bring my own chair, yeah?!'

From the next room came a loud BANG, followed by:

'That's not my milk!'

Maria took a drag from her pouch. 'Right, I'm going. I'm going to tell them about Tony.'

Martus grabbed her sleeve.

'No. You will not tell them we're from Deep. You will not tell them about Death. You will not say anything that sounds like a spell or a religious chant.'

'So what should I say?'

'That you're looking for... a relative. He went missing. He's a bit odd, charismatic, and possibly armed.'

Maria stood up, straightened her apron, which didn't even have pockets, although she still put her hands in them.

'I'm going.'

She walked slowly, carefully. Martus watched her. In his head, he prepared an excuse in case she got arrested.

But for now... she passed. No one shouted, no one pointed at her. She simply sat down across from a tired police officer who was chewing gum at a speed that could have torn through dimensions.

Maria leaned towards the desk and said, 'Good afternoon. We're looking for someone. He's around... eternity years old. Tall, pale, sometimes looks like he's talking to himself. Might have had a little figure with him.'

The police officer stopped chewing. She blinked. Slowly, like a computer from the 1990s.

Then she said, 'Take a seat. We'll be right with you.'

Martus sighed and sat down next to her after Maria turned with a triumphant smile.

'So far so good,' he muttered.

Maria sat rigidly. Knees together, hands on her lap, as though afraid someone might steal a biscuit from her pocket. Next to her sat Martus, his needles folded into a 'resting' position, but his foot tapped nervously, sounding like a ticking mechanical bomb.

A policeman sat across from them, leaning back in his chair with the kind of boredom that made no effort to hide itself. He was chewing on something, slow and noisy, like it was the only thing keeping him awake.

There was a crunch. Then a squeak. Another crunch. And a click.

Martus frowned.

'What is he doing?'

Maria leaned towards him, subtly.

'I don't know. Maybe... ruminating? Like a cow? Do humans do that?'

Martus opened the guidebook. 'Ruminating... ruminating... not listed.' He flipped through more pages. Then he read, 'Chewing gum. Human artefact. Purpose unclear. Consumed but must not be swallowed. Remains in mouth. Some flavours include mint, poisonous fruit, radioactive cherry.'

Maria frowned.

'Wait. They put something in their mouths that they're not supposed to swallow? And it smells like a deadly tree?'

Martus nodded.

'And they do it voluntarily.'

They fell silent. The policeman noticed they were staring at him. He slowed his chewing.

'Can I help you with something?' he asked cautiously.

Maria tapped the plastic divider between them.

'Excuse me, that thing in your mouth. Is that the… chewing substance made from gum and deadly flavours?'

The police officer blinked.

Martus pulled the guidebook closer.

'It says here that sometimes people stick it under tables. Is that true?'

The officer paused.

'Erm… yes. Yes, unfortunately.'

Maria froze.

'And why do you do that? Is it… a ritual? A summoning of demons? A mating season signal?'

'No, it's… just a bad habit.'

Martus turned to Maria.

'Bad habit,' he repeated solemnly. 'That translates as a deliberate destruction of hygiene and elegance.'

The officer burst out laughing.

'You two... is this some kind of hidden camera thing?'

Maria smiled.

'No. We're completely normal. We just have very thorough training in human observation.'

The officer leaned back in his chair and shook his head.

'I need to write this down. And I might have another piece of gum, because I really need it.'

Martus pulled out his notebook, written with old ink-thread.

'Chewing gum. Usage: stress response during encounters with unknown entities. Possibly useful for hostility assessment.'

Maria nodded.

'And apparently... for making friends too.'

Martus leaned towards the counter and cleared his throat as if about to make an official declaration from the Deep Council.

'We are looking for... a prince.'

The officer behind the desk looked up. Slowly. With suspicion.

'A prince?'

Maria nodded, her hairpins creaking.

'Yes. Young. About this tall. Polite. Slightly restless. Possibly with… erratic tendencies.'

Martus opened the guidebook and read aloud, 'Tonny. Son of Death. Prince of the Deep. Last known location: human world, souls, confusion, uncertainty. Possibly in danger.'

The officer removed his glasses.

'Hold on. Are you trying to tell me… you're looking for… the son of Death?'

'Yes,' they replied in unison.

'And you're saying you're from some place called… the Deep?'

Maria smiled.

'Yes. Deep. As in, so deep that even moles won't go there.'

The man at the desk slowly reached for the bell marked 'Psychiatric Department – crisis'.

Martus noticed and quickly pulled out a parchment.

'We also have a map. It's handwritten, and recognised by six infernal departments.'

'Please,' sighed the officer. 'This is a station, not Hogwarts. Do you have names? Surnames? Birth number? Anything that can be verified and does not wear a hood?'

And then a voice behind them said,

'Wait. Are you looking for Tonny?'

Martus turned. Maria held her breath.

An older man stood in the corner of the waiting room. With a face that looked like it had laughed once and had been trying to survive ever since.

'Are you... his people?'

Martus nodded slowly. His needles clicked softly.

'You know him?' Maria asked.

'Yeah. I was in a cell with him. He talked to himself. Said he was the son of Death. I thought he was mad...' he looked at them, '...but you look like the asylum that spawned him.'

Maria beamed. Martus sighed.

'And where is he now?' he asked quickly.

The man shrugged.

'An old guy took him. Tall. Straight as a pole. Had a stare that stripped you down to your soul. The police let him go because he said he was the lad's grandfather or something. They had his address... somewhere in the records.'

Martus and Maria looked at each other.

'We need that address,' said Martus. Slowly. Not as a request. But as if stating a direction of the universe.

The man chuckled.

'Well, you probably won't get it here. But the officer who spoke to him back then… he's on the night shift. Should be in soon.'

Maria sat back down on the bench.

'Alright. We'll wait. And in the meantime…' she pulled out a biscuit, '…I'll have something for the nerves.'

Martus simply added,

'And I'll start writing a report to the Deep. Title: Human logic – still non-existent.'

They sat on the bench in the corner of the station. Between them lay the manual, already well-thumbed, with a corner stained by butter sauce from their previous stop.

Maria crossed and uncrossed her legs nervously.

'You know,' she began, without looking at him, 'if I weren't in this mad situation, I'd probably have some cake now. Or tea. Or… cake in tea.'

Martus snorted. 'No tea for you! Anyway… If you weren't in this situation, you'd be back in the kitchen baking pastries that can burn both tongue and conscience.'

Maria smiled. 'And you'd be locked up in the workshop crying into your seams because no one loves you.'

'I don't cry. The needles rust.'

'Sure. And I'm not the best baker in three dimensions.'

They fell silent. Martus looked at her. She looked at him. Both pretending not to look.

'By the way…' Maria grinned, 'that officer keeps staring at you.'

'Because I have needles instead of hands, Maria. Not because I remind him of his first love.'

'Hm… pity. That back pocket of yours really does flatter those… well, legs.'

Martus nearly choked on his own tongue. 'My what?'

'Never mind. Just an observation. From a dough expert. You know. Er… shapes, texture, elasticity.'

Martus rolled his eyes. 'If we survive this, you're the first one I'm flattening.'

'Romantic as a bat thigh, Martus.'

And just then, the door opened.

The officer, the older one, with a stare that could burn through steel, walked in, a file under his arm, his expression serious.

'You're looking for the boy… the son of Death, aren't you?'

Both fell silent.

Maria froze. Martus gave a small nod.

The officer approached them, pulled out a sheet of paper, examined it briefly, then handed it to Martus.

'This is where they took him. An older man. Said to be his grandfather.'

Martus nodded. A quiet thank you. Maria simply smiled gently, her eyes glistening. When the officer left, Martus folded the paper and slipped it into his pocket.

They were silent for a while.

'We're going home,' Martus said softly.

'Well... off to find our little prince,' added Maria.

At the corner of his mouth came the usual faint smile, following a huff, when she slipped her hand onto his elbow with quiet willingness.

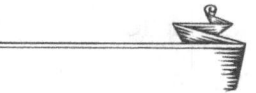

Chapter Twenty
I Should Know

We walked to her flat. She didn't say much, just kept moving like this was all normal. I followed, a step behind, trying not to look as completely lost as I felt. The street was narrow and smelled like concrete after rain, even though it hadn't rained. That bothered me. The flower shop downstairs had bright yellow flowers out front, fake looking, probably real. We climbed a staircase that tilted the wrong way. I think it was trying to escape.

The walls were too close together, and the handrail was warm from too many people who'd lived here before her. When she opened the door, I stopped in the frame. This was… it? Her flat. Not a guest suite, not a royal chamber, not even a cave you'd rest in while rebuilding your strength after battle. Just… this.

I stepped inside carefully, like the floor might shift under me. Everything was close. The ceiling dipped like it regretted its existence, and the walls were painted in that very specific shade of human compromise. The kind that says 'I wanted blue, but the shop had beige on sale.'

'Do you own this?' I asked, because that was the only explanation that made sense. Even if it wasn't much, it was hers, right?

She snorted across the room. 'God, no. I rent it.'

'You... rent it?'

As if it were obvious, she looked back at me over her shoulder.

'Yes. I pay money to live here. Every month. Welcome to Earth.'

There was a silence. It stretched between us like something had gone wrong with gravity.

'So you pay to stay in a room you don't own.'

'That's rent,' she said, already half in the kitchen. 'We've been doing it for a while.'

A sick, tight twist gripped the stomach, the feeling that comes when you realise the book you studied skipped the most important part. All those years reading about humans — their cities, their gods, their dramas and rituals — and not once had anyone told me about rent?

'This should have been in the studies,' I muttered. 'There were entire scrolls on bicycles. They gave me three hours on cheese. But rent? Nothing.'

'You're really stuck on this.'

'I should know. I'm supposed to understand your world. I was trained.'

She shrugged, pulling a mismatched mug from the cupboard. It had a strange shape, like it had been designed for a hand that didn't fully evolve.

'Study's not the same as living in it.'

That landed harder than I wanted it to. I glanced around again. There were shelves that looked ready to fall off the wall, a sofa with too many pillows, and a blanket that seemed permanently in the wrong place. The window was open but barely let in any air. Still, there was a smell — lavender, maybe, and something human I couldn't name. Dust and comfort and long nights.

'You live here,' I said, not as a question.

'Yeah.'

'And you feel safe in this box?'

She turned, met my eyes, and said, 'Safe enough.'

I walked a little further in. Touched a book on the shelf that was out of order. Looked at a small photo in a bent frame. Her and someone else, laughing into the blur of a cheap camera. I didn't know what to do with my hands. I sat down on the edge of the couch like it might push me back. It didn't. The pillow beside me had a face on it. I didn't ask why. I didn't want to know.

'I don't like it,' I said.

'You don't have to.'

'There's no space to think.'

'There's no space to hide, either. That's the point.'

That shut me up. She opened a cupboard and began throwing things into a rucksack. A jumper. Keys. Plums. (Plums?) I stood by the door, looking around like a child in a museum, unsure whether to sit down or lick everything.

'For the road,' she said, tossing me a plum.

I caught it. Looked at it. Then looked at her. 'Is this... a weapon or dinner?'

'Both,' she said with a smile.

And maybe... maybe there was something in that smile that hadn't been there before. Or maybe I just wanted it to be.

Someone stopped us in the hallway. Well, not exactly stopped. He bumped into my shoulder, hard enough to make a point but not enough to call it a fight. It was the kind of thing humans do when they want control without committing to conflict. Strange, really. In the Deep, you just say what you mean. 'Going somewhere?' he asked, all casual, like he just happened to be there by accident.

'Bad timing, was it?'

He was looking at me the entire time, not Lucy. Which felt off. Not threatening, just... wrong. He wore a ridiculous hat and looked about twenty, though there was something about him that made him seem less finished, somehow. Too clean, too pale. If we were in the Deep, I might have called him a milk-skin, but I already knew that wouldn't go down well in this world. That was one of the first things I'd learned. Keep your mouth shut, at least until you understand the rules.

'What do you want?' Lucy asked.

He glanced at me again, slowly, from top to bottom, and then turned back to her like I wasn't worth keeping in the conversation.

'Am I not allowed to visit my girlfriend?' he said. 'Or is this thing next to you yours now?' His tone was bitter, and the way he said thing made something tighten in my chest.

Lucy hesitated just a moment. Then she swallowed and lifted her head.

'He's my boyfriend,' she said clearly.

That surprised me. I wasn't her boyfriend. At least, I didn't think I was.

'I...' I tried to say something, but he spoke over me with the kind of smirk people use when they think they've already won.

'Yeah. Thought you had better taste.' Then he brushed some invisible dust off his jacket like that settled it, like he was still the one in control.

And that got under my skin. Was he talking about me? Did he mean I wasn't enough? That I didn't measure up? He had no idea who I was. I wasn't just some stranger in a hallway. I was Tonny, prince of the Deep, the only son of Death. The most beautiful, too, probably. I'd been told that often enough. I stepped forward, but before I could speak,

Lucy cut in.

'Move,' she said. 'We're leaving.'

She took my hand, her grip stronger than I expected, and gave him a shove with her shoulder as we passed. He didn't take it well. He grabbed her wrist.

'You bitch,' he shouted.

I didn't think. I didn't need to. I hit him. Not because he insulted me. I didn't care about that. But because where I come from, you do not lay hands on a woman in anger. If we'd been back home, he wouldn't have had time to regret it. He wouldn't have had a tongue left. He spun as he fell and landed hard.

I looked at Lucy. She smiled, just a little, and I felt something shift in me. Not pride. Not triumph. Just the quiet sense that maybe, in that moment, I'd done the right thing. I took her hand again, and we walked toward the door. I didn't know what had passed between them. I wasn't sure if he had been her boyfriend, or if something worse had happened there. Maybe both.

I'd studied human behaviour as best I could, but this part, the part where things stopped being said out loud, still confused me. What I did understand was the way her hand held mine, the way her face looked calmer now than it had a moment before. And in that silence, I knew she felt safer.

We stepped outside. Her car was an old Škoda. A bit rusty, a bit charismatic, but it smelled of petrol and regrets. I sat in the passenger seat and watched her start the engine. It ran. Well — it roared and prayed, but it ran. We were quiet for a while. And I thought about the fact that I was sitting in a human car. With a human woman. No protection, no power, no plan. And somehow... I wanted to cry.

But instead, I just rested my head against the window and said quietly, 'You know... it was my dream to come here. To this world.'

Lucy didn't answer right away. She looked at me like she was trying to figure out if I meant it.

'Well,' she said finally, 'your dream came true.' There was a pause. Then she added, softer, 'Are you happy?'

'Yeah. I've got a missing father, a stolen Roddy, and people who think I'm a cosplayer with a reality disorder.'

Lucy laughed. And that... calmed me a little. Then came the question. Not forced, but quiet enough to tell me it mattered.

'Do you have someone?'

I smiled. 'Yeah. Amalia.'

'I see.'

'She's... from Hell.'

'Hell?'

'Yes, she is daughter of Satan.'

'You really know how to pick them.'

'And the rules say we shouldn't be together.'

She went quiet. Then said, 'And do you follow rules?'

I turned my head back to the window. Trees. Houses. People. And me, somewhere in between.

'I've followed everything. Until now.'

'What's it like... there? Up? Or down?' she asked, eyes on the road.

'Why does everyone say up or down?' I sighed. 'It's neither. We're... in between.'

'I see.'

'Well, whatever,' I said. 'Anyway... it's beautiful there. Now that I'm here, I really see it. Our world, our palace, everything... it was actually beautiful. I just never realised it. I kept dreaming of getting here among people. Because I'm half human, you know?'

'I understand… well, that's impressive.'

I shrugged. She smiled. Then I leaned slightly towards her.

'And you? I mean, he was your boyfriend? No kids? I mean… most women your age usually have some. I mean… based on what I studied.'

Lucy burst out laughing. And not in a polite way — in a what the hell did you just say kind of way.

'You studied that?'

I hesitated. 'Well, yes. Not in depth… but we've got volumes on it. Human biology, reproductive cycles, cultural norms. One of the demons lectured us. He was… very detailed.'

Her laughter didn't fade. It shifted into that quiet kind of laugh that makes you laugh with her.

'And you're telling me that you… you and Amalia…'

I frowned. 'What? Kids? No. Only after marriage, obviously.'

'Of course…' she said. And in her voice there was something… gentle. Maybe a smile, maybe softness. Maybe a hint of envy. But she hid it quickly. As always. She was a kind human. That much I knew. I smiled, then turned back to the window. The world outside moved past in quiet shapes and colours. I was just starting to let myself feel calm again when something hit us. It wasn't loud or dramatic. Just sudden. A jolt from the side, heavy and clumsy. The car tilted slightly. Lucy shouted something, sharp and quick, but I didn't catch the words. The wheel spun in her hands. I felt the tyres pull hard against the road, and then we stopped. Everything went still. For a few seconds, neither of us moved. The sound had drained out of the world, and all I could hear was the tight, uneven rhythm of my own breath.

Then Lucy's whisper.

'Oh, bloody hell…'

She ran out. I stayed with the plum stone, breathing steady, certain of what had happened. Then I stepped out slowly. People stood nearby. One was pulling out a phone. Another stared elsewhere. A girl was crying. The car that had hit us was no longer in sight. A man lay on the ground. Lucy knelt beside him, her hand at his wrist. She already had her phone in the other hand. I didn't look at her hands. I didn't move toward the body. My eyes had already gone somewhere else.

Across the pavement, a little further down the street, just past the tree on the corner. Someone was standing there. He was tall and lean, dressed in a long black coat that hung still despite the breeze. His posture hadn't changed in all the years I remembered him. He looked exactly the same. Not younger, not older. Just... fixed, like time didn't apply to him the way it did to the rest of us. My grandfather Alfonzo came from the Deep. Empty-handed, silent, calm, he smiled faintly at the man on the ground. He had come for him.

It made sense. He had taken the work again. After Father left, after everything crumbled, he had returned to it. Death was needed here, and so he had come. When he came forward, I looked up, and for that short moment our eyes met. There was nothing in them but recognition.

A nod between two people who both knew how this was meant to go, and that it hadn't. This was meant to be mine. That was the truth of it. I had been raised for it, trained. Prepared, and yet it was him standing there, not me. At the ground he crouched and reached, and his hand filled with stillness. He let the woman go first, then followed her out of the world.

They walked past as if he wasn't there. I was the only one who saw. I stood there a while longer, heart thudding against something I didn't have a name for. Then I turned and walked toward Lucy, still not entirely sure what had just happened — only that I wasn't part of it. She was kneeling beside the man. Her hand still on his.

'Tonny... he...'

I saw Lucy's pain, though I didn't understand why. He was just gone... I had thought that now death had returned to the Earth, people would be happy. But they were sad. She didn't need to finish; she just sat there with her eyes turned down, and in them I saw something like glass breaking, not with a crash but in that quiet way that can never be repaired.

Her fingers still clung to him, and when I laid my palm gently on her shoulder. It hurts. That was what I realised, maybe for the first time, when I began to understand what death means for people.

We sat beside him. The man who had died. Lucy kept her hands on her knees, fingers clenched so tightly it looked like she was holding something invisible, something fragile that might slip through if she loosened her grip even slightly. She didn't speak. Neither did I. I stared at his shoes. They were brown, scuffed at the toes, with the left lace hanging loose like it had been stepped on more than once.

They reminded me of nothing in particular, yet somehow of everything at once. Shoes, and behind them a person, and behind that a quiet ending no one would ever bother to write down. No lightning split the sky, no shadow touched the ground. A life ended. I refused to look at his face. We stayed there for a while. Time didn't press on us, no words passed between us, only the heavy silence of a moment that seemed uncertain of itself.

Then Lucy spoke, her voice careful.

'What's it like... where you're from?'

I looked up and slowly met her eyes.

'Like what?'

'Death. In the Deep. What's it like when... someone dies there?'

I shrugged.

'Normal,' I said at last.

'Normal?'

'Yeah. Death is… like a transfer. Like finishing work and going home.'

Lucy was quiet. Staring ahead.

'So nobody cries?'

'No.'

'And you… you've never cried?'

I thought for a moment.

'No.'

I said it aloud, I wasn't sure if that was a good thing or not.

Lucy rubbed her eyes with the back of her hand.

'You know, I didn't even know him. That man… I mean. But it still felt like… like something was ripped out. Not mine. But… out of the space. The air.'

I nodded.

'Where I'm from… death doesn't rip. It stitches back into order., into silence.'

We sat quietly for a while. Then Lucy said, 'I don't want to die.'

Looking at her I realised it wasn't shock at all, but a kind of respect.

'Nobody does. But we all have to.'

'In the Deep, nobody talks about it.'

'Well, lucky you.'

Then she looked at me and raised an eyebrow.

'And you? Do you want to die one day, Tonny?'

I smiled faintly.

'Me? I don't even know if I can.'

'That's fair.'

For a while we just stared ahead. The car was still parked. The world moved around us, slowly, as if afraid to go any faster.

'Come on,' she said softly. 'Let's go.'

I stood. Looked one last time at the body.

'Alfonzo was quick.'

'Who?'

'My grandfather.'

'The one... you saw?'

'Yes.'

'And did you... say anything to him?'

'No. I just understood that he's working now.'

We got back in the car. And when we drove off, we didn't know much more than before. But we were quieter. I was sure. Not a 'maybe' kind of sure. Not a 'perhaps it's just a plum in the bag' feeling. No. This was him. Roddy. And he was close.

'Stop,' I said. 'Here. We're close now.'

Lucy didn't argue. She simply slowed down and looked at me, as if waiting for me to explain what I felt. But I didn't know. It just felt like… home. Like hearing a familiar voice in the dark. Roddy was calling me. I spilled out of the car before she had properly parked. We passed a few fruit stalls, a boy whistling on a plastic whistle, and then I saw it. A pawn shop. Broken sign, grimy window, and inside enough clutter to lose Death himself between a hoover and a battered teapot.

At the door I slipped in first, Lucy following after. The bell above gave its faint ring, and then it came to me: that had to be Roddy.

'He's here. He has to be,' I breathed.

'What?' Lucy didn't understand.

'Roddy.'

The man behind the counter came first to my notice: bald, thick fingers, a jumper with a hole in it. I hadn't waited but had gone directly to him. He looked as if he could sleep standing.

'I want the figurine,' I said.

The man looked up from a tiny television.

'What figurine? And by the way, hello? Ever heard of basic manners? Mean anything to you?'

'Excuse me? Do you know who I am? I'm the prince of the Deep.'

'Right. And I'm the king of the bee nest.'

'The king of bees? My apologies, Your Majesty,' I said, and gave a graceful bow. Respect is important.

The man turned to Lucy. She twirled her finger beside her temple. Then he smiled, and something shifted in his posture. I had no idea what she did, but somehow it worked. Suddenly he was cooperative. For a so-called king, he was actually quite a decent gentleman. He nodded towards the back with a jerk of his chin.

'A guy came in. Paid a fortune and laughed like a lunatic. Said the folks at the Burtura club would be glad to have it.'

'Burtura club?'

'Yeah. Wore glasses... a scarf. Came in like a bloke, left like a lord.'

My heart sped up a little.

'Do you have an address?'

'I don't keep an address book, lad. This is a pawn shop, not a ministry.'

I wanted to say a few things to him, but Lucy laid a hand on my shoulder, and I held back, standing there with my eyes fixed on the hole in his jumper.

'But you know what?' said the king, suddenly. 'Burtura's a pub. Not far. About three blocks from here.'

I nodded and gave a quick bow in thanks before we stepped outside again.

Chapter Twenty-one
The Pub That Smelled

The pub, smelling of sweat, pressed in around us. Its dim lighting made the room feel small and far away at once. Behind us, the door slammed shut with a thud. Lucy walked close behind me, her hands deep in her pockets and her head down. She looked like she already understood what kind of place this was.

I looked around; the pool table was chipped, the bar carried long cracks, and the men standing nearby hardly moved yet seemed to own the room simply by being there. They were large, with broad shoulders and worn leather jackets. With their boots planted wide apart, they didn't care who heard their loud laughter. This should have been the kind of place where I felt out of place.

But I didn't. What I noticed was the coldness; not a head turned, not a step slowed, not a glance in my direction, as though I didn't exist. Where I come from, in the Deep, names matter. People feel who you are before you speak. Here I was, just another stranger, no prince and no heir of Death, only someone passing through.

Where six men were drinking and smoking, I walked over to a table. They had large, scarred hands and dull eyes. I stopped and spoke.

'Excuse me. Do you know if someone brought in a small black figurine? About ten centimetres high. Cracked. Recently sold.'

There was a pause. A chair creaked. One man with stubble looked up slowly.

'What?'

I repeated the question. For a moment, no one said anything. Then someone laughed under his breath. Another man cleared his throat. A louder voice called out from across the room.

'Oi, what's with this poof?'

The word meant nothing. It was just thrown out to get a reaction. No one had ever spoken to me like that before, not in the Deep. There, respect is the rule. Here, it seemed optional. I didn't reply. I stared at the man until he looked uncomfortable. Then I took his wrist. My grip was firm, not violent, but enough for him to remember.

'You just touched a member of the royal family,' I said.

He hissed and pulled away. Chairs scraped and more men stood up. I let go of his wrist and stepped back.

'We can begin, if you want to.'

The first man rushed me too slowly, and I dropped him with a strike to the jaw. The next swung, but I slipped aside and hit his ribs twice. He staggered. A third swung a chain, and I pushed him forward to the floor. Quietly, a moment passed. Then five or six more came, one with a stool, another with a tray. I let them crash into each other. The stool splintered on the bar.

A fist caught my face, but I punched back and sent the man into the jukebox, which burst into a country tune before cutting out. Another tried, but I caught him with my elbow to the jaw.

He fell.

They all fell, strong but reckless. I stayed calm, using their weight against them. When it ended, the room was silent. Some men groaned on the floor. The rest froze, drinks in hand, unsure what came next.

I fixed my sleeve and brushed off my jacket. Then, there was a change in the air. A man stepped out from the shadows. A long grey coat hung from his shoulders, pale hair above, pale eyes beneath. The likeness to my father was striking, yet this was not Death. This was Pain, my cousin.

'Hello,' he said, in a quiet voice that carried through the room. Everyone froze. That was how Pain worked. You understood him only when he was close.

'You started without me?' he asked. 'I was busy. Break-ups, accidents, kidneys failing.'

A bottle slipped behind the bar and smashed.

'They started it,' I said. 'I just wanted a figurine.'

Pain nodded.

'Do you want help or should I just watch?'

'Watch, if you want. Maybe explain who I am.'

Pain smiled.

Another man charged. I dropped him with one hit. Pain lifted his hand, and the man screamed. More men came. Some I fought. Some Pain touched. They all fell. Then someone at the back spoke.

'I saw the man. He had the figurine. Said he worked in television. Wore a suit. Went to Club Neon.'

I nodded. Pain put his gloves back on.

'I'll find Father,' I said.

'Good. I prefer heartbreaks to bar fights.'

He disappeared. Lucy stepped forward from the back wall. She had been watching the whole time.

'You're mad,' she said.

'Thank you,' I replied.

I fixed my jacket and turned to leave.

'Come on. Roddy is waiting.'

Chapter Twenty-two
Old Man at Work

'Smells like… burnt toast and panic,' noted Martus, pulling up his coat collar.

Maria waved a hand in front of her nose. 'This London. I thought it'd be more… more… what's the guide say… civilised.'

'According to the guide, yes. But according to the nose, no.'

They walked on. The street was full of people, shop windows, car horns. And one bloke who just fell.

Out of nowhere. Onto his side. With a crunch and a look that said, 'Bloody hell, didn't see that coming.'

Maria stepped slightly around his body, like skirting a puddle.

'Probably slipped.'

Martus didn't even look. 'Local geology case.'

As they turned the corner, Martus lifted his head. Across the street, someone was standing motionless. The figure was tall, upright, wrapped in a coat the colour of night fog. When their eyes met, something settled in his chest. He knew those eyes — the quiet confidence, the stillness that didn't need explanation.

It was Alfonzo.

Martus just nodded. 'Old man at work.'

'Who's he taking?' asked Maria.

'The one who fell.'

'Ah.' A moment of silence. 'Y'know, they really don't fall stylishly here. In the Deep, we at least fall with a sound effect.'

'Sometimes even with lights.'

They carried on as if nothing had happened. Martus sniffed at a hot-dog stand and pulled a disgusted face.

'Smells like warm horsemeat.'

'Might be warm horsemeat,' replied Maria, pulling out the guide.

She flicked through it. 'Page 89 – Hot dog is not a dog. Right, progress.'

'Martus, ask someone.'

'Why me?'

'Because when I ask, they look like I've got a virus.'

'You've just got bad energy.'

'You mean I've got a bad face.'

'No, you've got a... beautiful face,' Martus said.

Marta blushed and smiled, looking away just slightly.

'Oh, stop it, you,' she said, trying not to laugh.

They stopped outside a shop with a front window so polished it almost looked like water. When they stepped inside, the bell above the door gave a quiet chime, and a new world opened around them.

The effort was clear: someone had worked hard with starch, wax, and pine to make the place smell untouched by time. The floor gleamed. Heavy curtains framed the corners. Along the walls, black-and-white photographs showed stern men in stiff suits, standing so straight it felt like train tracks could have run along their spines.

Taking it in silently, Martus shifted the edge of his coat, as though gauging the room's temperature or its mood. Behind the counter stood a woman. She looked around forty, maybe a little older, but she wore her age like something carefully chosen. There was nothing out of place. Not the line of her hair, not the shape of her posture. Even the curve of her hand on the wood seemed practiced.

And then she saw them.

She didn't freeze because of Maria. It was Martus who held her gaze. Something about him made her pause, as if he was a memory she couldn't quite place, or a name she didn't realise she'd forgotten. Slowly, she stepped out from behind the counter. Without a word. And then… she reached out her hand.

Martus flinched. Just slightly.

'May I?' she asked quietly.

She didn't wait for him to say anything. Just reached for his hand, for the needles. Her fingers brushed over one carefully, like she wasn't sure if it would snap or stab her.

'That is… stunning,' she breathed. 'You're… real?'

'Unfortunately,' muttered Martus.

She ran her finger along the threads. Thin, tight, precise.

'This… this is art. Not a tool. This is… fate.'

Martus blinked.

Maria stood a little behind them, hands on hips. At first startled. Then a few centimetres closer.

The woman leaned in towards Martus. Closer still.

'Where did you learn to construct like this? That sort of… ratio?'

Maria stepped forward.

'Excuse me,' she said, far too loudly. 'Don't know if it's occurred to you, but this isn't a display. This is my... this is Martus.'

The woman leaned back slightly, but her hand stayed on Martus's wrist.

'I apologise,' she said without a hint of remorse. 'It's just not something you see every day.'

'Too right,' growled Maria. 'And when you do, you don't cling to it like dough on a bad baking tray.'

Martus slowly backed off. The needles clicked. He stepped away from the admirer and straightened his collar.

'The house,' he reminded her flatly. 'Address.'

The woman genuinely regretted it. Then pointed toward the window.

'Two streets down, on the right. White door. If that's who you're looking for... there.'

Martus nodded. Maria was already at the door.

Outside, they paused.

'I'll tell you something,' muttered Maria.

'Hm?'

'If anyone else touches your needles... I'll sew them a cloak. From their own skin.'

Martus stayed silent, his mouth twitching. The street was quiet, broken by a car, a bike bell, and a bird screeching. Martus stopped in front of the white door, but Maria didn't. She walked a little further, stopping by a low fence. On the other side, a small child was playing on the grass. Round-cheeked, focused entirely on a melting ice cream, wearing the kind of happiness you only get when life hasn't introduced you to bills or deadlines.

'Oh God... it's a child!' gasped Maria.

Martus rolled his eyes.

'Brilliant.'

'Look at it! Those eyes! Those little hands!'

'Yeah yeah. Tiny humans. All they do is pee everywhere. Come on.'

Maria stayed by the fence, leaning on it. The child looked at her, licked the ice cream, then fell on its bum and started laughing.

'Martus...' said Maria softly, and glanced at him, 'remember when Tonny was little?'

Martus froze. Frowned. Slung his bag over his shoulder.

'I remember. I also remember he peed in flowerpots, shoes, drawers, and once on the council table.'

Maria laughed. Louder than she meant to. But then sobered, still looking at the child. And for a moment, just for a moment… something strange in her eyes. Not sadness. More like… maybe, one day...

Where he stood, Martus shifted, muttering under his breath once he noticed, 'If you start talking about baby muffins, I'm walking home.'

Maria finally turned and smiled.

'You'd manage to get as far as the ditch.'

They walked up to the door together. It was white, the paint peeling, and the letterbox hung slightly crooked, like it had given up trying to hold itself straight. Martus reached out and knocked.

'Do you think he's in?' whispered Maria.

Martus knocked again in silence. This time the door shifted, inch by inch, the sound it made closer to memory than to wood.

A man stood behind the door. Older, in a worn dressing gown. His hair was white, but there was strength in the way he held himself. His eyes were sharp and focused, as if they had already measured everything in front of him. His face was unreadable, a mug of coffee steady in one hand. He offered no words, only his gaze. After that, they looked back. It was not tense quiet; it was more like a pause, as if both sides were still deciding how much of themselves to show.

'What are you lot?' he said at last. Deep voice. Like someone reading from memory.

Martus already had the answer ready, reaching into his coat for a folded piece of paper worn thin at the edges, the address itself, which he handed over without a word.

'We… we're looking for Tonny.'

The man took the paper. Looked at it like he was meant to eat it.

'And why do you think he's here?' he asked.

'Because we talked to a gentleman at the police station who said you took him out of the cell,' added Maria, trying to sound natural, even though she wanted to both hug and punch the old man at the same time.

The old man nodded, calm as ever, and then stepped aside.

'Come in, then.'

They entered the hallway like two people unsure whether you were meant to keep your shoes on or bow to the floor. Martus stopped just inside the door, arms stiff at his sides, his needle-fingers gently clinking against the fabric. His eyes moved across the wall, taking in the photos. Human moments, caught and framed, time pinned behind glass. He looked at them carefully, but didn't quite understand what they were meant to hold.

Quietly excited, Maria brushed her hand over the curtain and leaned toward the flower in the vase to smell it. The curtain fascinated her more than the light outside. They didn't have curtains back home, or flowers that were dead but still smelled alive.

'This is where we sit,' said the old man, nodding towards the living room.

Martus went first, the wooden floor creaking slightly beneath his steps, and he stopped by an armchair as if waiting for instructions. Maria followed at once, sitting on the very edge of the sofa with her hands folded in her lap and her apron smoothed neatly across her knees.

The old man sat opposite, in his own chair, and looked at them for a long time.

He didn't ask anything straight away, just drank his coffee, then sighed.

'You're not people.'

Martus raised an eyebrow.

'What makes you say that?' he asked slowly.

'Needles instead of hands, the young lady in an apron in the middle of the week, and that look on your faces. Like your universe broke but you're still trying to be polite.'

Maria smiled proudly.

'We're looking for Tonny,' she said quietly. 'He's our... prince.'

The old man nodded.

'I know who Tonny is. And you two look like the kind who'd walk through hell for him.'

Maria blushed. Martus didn't even blink.

'And you're already nearly there,' added the old man. Then he stood up. 'Do you want tea? Or something… less British?'

Maria opened her mouth, but Martus cut in first. 'Got anything that doesn't fizz, hiss or come from chocolate?'

The old man laughed for the first time.

'I've got water,' he said, standing from his chair.

'Thank you,' Martus replied quietly.

As the old man poured hot water into the mugs, a sharp and unfamiliar smell filled the room, a scent that belonged nowhere in the Deep. Maria bent forward to test it with a cautious sniff, but she recoiled almost instantly, coughing into her apron.

'Sorry,' she said, wiping her nose. 'This… this tea, we cannot.'

The old man gave a small smile as he sat back down.

'Why's that?'

Martus didn't touch his mug. He stared into it instead. One of his needles twitched slightly as he said, 'We are politely refusing your tea.'

'No problem,' the old man said with a shrug.

Martus looked at him more directly. 'So anyway. Where is Tonny?'

'He went to find Roddy,' the old man answered.

Martus frowned. 'Roddy… and where?'

'I don't know exactly,' the old man said. 'But I'm sure Tonny is doing fine. He's a good man, and smart.'

Maria nodded. 'Of course he is. He's my little cutie pie.'

The old man turned to her, eyes curious. 'And you are?'

Maria raised her chin slightly.

'I was about to ask you the same,' she said calmly, while Martus kept his eyes on the steam rising from the mug.

'I'm his grandfather,' the old man said.

Martus blinked. 'Grandfather?'

'Yes,' the man said. 'And why have you both come here?'

Martus shifted slightly in his seat.

'He took over. Alan. He says the Deep needs a new order. Peace. A cleanup after Death's reign.'

The old man's face didn't move much, but something in his eyes tightened.

'And what about your prince?' he asked. 'Tonny?'

Martus paused.

'He sent him,' he said at last. 'To become something else.'

The old man watched him.

'A human?' he asked.

No one answered right away.

Maria nodded. 'In five days. Then he'll never come back.'

The moment was quiet, a spoon tapping porcelain the only noise. Then the telly started up, and the old man turned.

'I didn't even touch it.'

'I definitely didn't,' said Maria.

On the screen, the logo of some morning show blinked into view, too bright for the hour. The shot cut to a studio with soft colours, polished smiles, and two presenters arranged just so.

And between them, placed neatly on a cushion like some prize on display, was Roddy. He wasn't moving, but he was clearly alive. Every angle of the camera caught him just right. He gleamed under the lights, practically sparkled.

The camera didn't just show him. It loved him.

'...a unique object that experts in magic – and ordinary people – believe in...'

'I got him a few days ago from a small pawn shop,' said the suited man next to them. 'I believe he can change moods... space... maybe even reality.'

Maria started coughing. Martus stood up.

'We have to go.'

The old man was already on his feet too.

'Tonny loved him,' he just said. 'He was his... friend.'

'If Roddy's there,' added Maria, 'Tonny won't be far.'

The old man reached for his coat.

'I'm coming with you.'

'No,' said Martus. 'But thank you.'

The old man was quiet for a while, then just nodded.

'Alright. But take this.' He pulled a small key from his pocket. 'To my old car. It's not fast, but it has soul.'

They paused at the door.

Maria turned back once more. 'Thank you. For the tea.'

'For Tonny,' Martus corrected gently.

They opened the door to leave. But the old man collapsed. There was no dramatic fall, no cry for help. Just a soft sound, like a book slipping off the edge of a sofa.

Martus turned half a second too late and looked down.

'Well. That's that,' he said.

Maria leaned over the body and poked his cheek with a finger. Nothing.

'Hmmm. Dead as a doorknob.'

'Okay, let's go,' Martus said, already halfway through the doorway.

But Maria reached out and stopped him with a hand on his shoulder.

'But... he's Tonny's grandfather. Should we do something?'

Martus rolled his eyes, sighed, and muttered, 'Fine.' He then shrugged, pulled out the guidebook, and flipped to the chapter with the discreet title: *'What to do when someone pops their clogs (and there's no time for drama)'*

Maria, meanwhile, dragged over a stool, sat down next to the old man's body, and started cleaning her nails.

'Fancy a tea?' she called, like she was talking about the weather.

'Tea? You want to die?'

'Course. Always wanted a funeral brew. Deep classic.'

'Shush, woman!' Martus then read aloud. 'First point: In the event of an unexpected death in the human realm, do not panic. Corpses do not explode.'

'That's good to know,' muttered Maria, kicking the old man's shoe that had fallen off.

'Second point: Confirm that the person is really dead. It is recommended to speak to them, nudge gently, or lightly dust with flour.'

Martus glanced at the kitchen counter.

'You got flour?'

'I've got semolina.'

'That'll do.'

They sprinkled semolina on the old man's forehead.

Nothing.

'Alright. Onto point three.'

'Bury him?'

'Bury him.'

Out in the garden, it was a circus. Martus dug. His needles vibrated with frustration as he hit a root. Maria held an empty flowerpot and tried to figure out where they could plant the old man like a tree.

'It says here: the grave must meet the aesthetic standards of human cemeteries.'

'Meaning what?' she asked.

'It has to be level. And no socks sticking out.'

Maria nodded. 'Right. Call me when the hole's ready. I'm off to make the headstone.'

She disappeared for a while, and when she came back, she was holding a bit of a biscuit tin with the words written in marker: *HERE LIES OLD MAN. NO STEPPING.*

Martus gave her a look. 'Seriously?'

'Oi, better than nothing.'

They wrapped the old man in a blanket with bears on it (Maria couldn't find another one) and quietly lowered him down.

'Well then… goodnight, Old Man.'

They stood in silence for a moment.

Then Maria carefully placed a bread roll next to the grave.

'In case he gets hungry.'

Martus nodded.

'I'd add garlic. In case he comes back.'

And then they left without looking back.

Because in the Deep, death is just Monday. Bit crap, but no reason to cancel the plan.

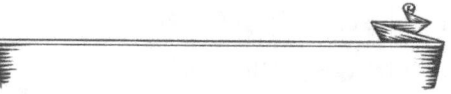

Chapter Twenty-three
We're Somewhere in Between

The car was quiet. The engine hummed, and the wipers slid across the glass now and then. Lucy was behind the wheel, hands steady, eyes fixed on the road. She didn't speak. That wasn't a good sign. I sat next to her with ash on my trousers, glass in my sleeve, and some kind of sauce on my shoe that wasn't part of the plan.

'Um, have you been working out?' she asked. Calm voice.

'Working out? No. Never needed to. In the Deep, we don't really do that. It's a human thing. But I studied it.'

'Right. Well, just saying, you took out thirty guys without breaking a sweat. You were chatting to someone I couldn't even see, and now you're sitting here like you've had a massage.'

I shrugged.

'I keep telling people. I'm a prince from the Deep. When are you all going to believe me?'

'Well now I do. I bow to you, Prince of the Deep.'

'That's how it should be.'

She laughed, but it wasn't really about anything funny. It was nerves.

'I thought you were just strange. Maybe a lot strange. But now I think I'm the crazy one for not kicking you out of the car already.'

She glanced at me, and I couldn't read her face. Some people are just hard to read. Amelia was like that too.

'Who was that? The one I couldn't see?'

'My cousin.'

'Right. And what is he?'

'Pain.'

She paused.

'You mean his name? A title?'

'No. Pain. Real pain. It's his role. A job.'

'So... you Deep people. You're the ones causing pain to humans?'

'Not exactly. Not from down there. Not from up there either. We're somewhere in between.'

'Yeah, well, forget it.'

She looked like she wanted to ask more, but stopped herself. She kept driving, which was fine by me. I needed quiet. I hadn't realised how slow humans were. In the Deep, I never had to fight. No one dared.

What happened earlier was stupid. Outrageous, even. Humans were loud and shameless. No wonder Hell was rich. There was sin everywhere. Even though I wasn't fully human and hadn't yet inherited everything, I was still royal.

I had been born fast and strong, and everyone knew what that meant. No one was supposed to touch me, yet they had, and one day they would pay for it. If I turned into Death, I would take care of it myself, hoping they would remember.

Lucy started singing then, not well but loud, something about love and flying and citrus fruit.

The radio was blasting.

'What is this torture?' I muttered, pulling my hood over my ears.

'It's Dua Lipa, you ignoramus,' she said, and turned it up.

'Sounds like a spell.'

She laughed, pulled one hand off the wheel, grabbed her phone, and dropped it in my lap.

'Put something on, prince of the Deep. Red icon. YouTube. Go on.'

I stared at the screen. Then tapped. It lit up with colours, thumbnails, and titles. I typed: old music from the world. First result: some man with a guitar singing about his cat leaving him, followed by his girlfriend.

Not knowing what I was meant to feel, I kept scrolling until the screen stopped on a studio couch under bright lights. Two presenters sat at either side, and between them was Roddy, awake and talking, smiling as if it were the most normal thing in the world.

The camera stayed on him like he was the most important thing in the room. The caption said: Miracle figurine: is it magic or a hoax? I felt my chest tighten. Not fear. Just the clear sense that something had changed.

'Stop,' I said.

'What?'

'I said stop. Now. We know where he is.'

Lucy leaned in to look at the phone. Her face shifted. She looked focused.

'Right. We know where he is,' she said.

Then she floored it. No warning. No signal. The car launched forward.

'Wait— what are you doing?' I grabbed the dashboard.

'We're going to get Roddy. You think he'll stay on TV forever?'

'You just overtook an ambulance!'

'It didn't have the lights on. It's legal.'

'That's not legal!'

We shot through a junction. I couldn't even tell what colour the lights were anymore. Lucy was laughing and singing. She overtook everything. My face was pressed to the window.

'Lucy, you're—'

'Yeah?'

'You're a psychopath.'

'Thanks. That's the nicest thing anyone's said to me today.'

We passed a giant cake billboard. I think sugar exploded.

'My insides hurt.'

'Tonny, relax. You're from the Deep. Your dad's Death. You can handle a little car ride.'

'This isn't a ride. This is death on wheels.'

She skidded into an alley. The car bounced. I thought I was going to die before Death even got the chance. Then she slowed down. Finally.

We stopped outside a large building. Neon sign: LTV Studios. She looked at me.

'See? You're still breathing. Now go get your magical mate.'

Shaky but smiling, I had no idea why. It might have been because she drove across half the city for a toy, or because, even after nearly killing us, I felt more alive beside her than I ever had in the Deep. I tried to get out first, but my body didn't respond right. It wasn't sudden. Just heavy. Heat spread through me. My stomach turned. It wasn't the drive. It was something else. Lucy was already outside, saying something, but her voice sounded far away. Stepping out and trying to act normal, I realised something was wrong. My body no longer felt mine; pins and needles spread in my hands, pressure rose in my head, my heartbeat altered, and I leaned on the car for support.

'Tonny?' Lucy asked. She was close now.

I looked up and tried to smile. 'It's nothing. Maybe I needed more air.'

'Your hands are shaking. Sit down. Now.'

'No, really, I—' Then it hit me. My stomach twisted. I bent forward. Breathing hard didn't help. Something inside me was shifting. Not outside. Inside. Deep.

'I'm calling an ambulance,' Lucy said, pulling out her phone.

'I'll be fine. It'll pass,' I whispered. But I knew it wouldn't.

She was already talking. 'Yes, I've got someone here. He's unwell. I need an ambulance. It's urgent.' Then she froze.

'What happened?' I asked.

'They said they're overloaded. Too many calls. People are dying.' She looked at me. Calm, not afraid. 'Death is back.'

I nodded, already knowing, yet the words still struck me hard. I was changing, not into something new but into something human, and the change was slow, quiet, and unstoppable. Because the shaking in my body had ended, I sat on the car bonnet with hands on my knees, still feeling unsettled within. Not fear, but the heavy aftermath of what had happened.

Then a warm smell reached me, butter and bread, something ordinary and comforting. I looked up to see Lucy beside me with a paper bag in her hands. She didn't speak, only offered it, and I raised an eyebrow before taking it from her. Inside lay a sandwich with butter, egg, and lettuce.

Nothing special. But when I bit into it, I felt something ease. My shoulders dropped. My thoughts quieted. It wasn't magic, only food, only care. I leaned back and looked at her, though she kept her eyes elsewhere, and she didn't need to meet mine because the silence between us was enough.

Something moved in the mirror, a blur at first that soon grew clear. A black car pulled up behind us, polished and shining. Another followed, then a third, each one stopping in perfect line. Their doors opened together and tall figures stepped out in long coats and clean shoes, moving without haste. One paused to glance around while another walked to the studio door and knocked twice. I stayed still and watched.

The way they moved stood out right away. It was familiar. Controlled. Every step was exact. Every movement had purpose. I knew what it was. Training. Focus. The kind we were raised with. They were from the Deep.

'Lucy,' I whispered.

She leaned in. 'What?'

'They're mine.'

She followed my eyes.

'You mean... from the Deep? And is that good?'

I didn't answer right away. I wasn't sure. Had they come for me? Or for Roddy? I pulled my hood up.

'We're leaving.'

'I thought —'

'Change of plan.'

We got back in the car. Before the door shut, I looked back. I saw them disappear inside the studio. That's how they came. That's how I'll leave too.

Chapter Twenty-four
Automobiles

They stood by the car.

'This is the machine?' Maria frowned. 'Doesn't look dangerous. But usually it's things like this that eat your soul.'

'Maria? We don't have souls, so it's safe for us,' said Martus, holding the keys and waving them in the air as though testing whether they would activate any magic. 'It's a transport device. Chapter thirteen. 'Vehicles. Automobiles. Not to be confused with funeral vehicles, which usually do not move on their own.''

'Right. Fine,' Maria nodded and crouched by the door like it was an oven. 'And how does this… open?'

'Press that button. The symbol… looks like a door, or maybe an open trap.'

Maria pressed it, and when the car blinked, she jumped. 'It's doing that on purpose.'

Martus opened the door and gestured inside. 'Sit there. On the driver's throne.'

Maria sat down. The seat hissed.

'Martus… it's breathing.'

'No. That's you.'

'Ah.'

Martus walked around the car slowly, cautiously, like it might bite. He got in beside her, guidebook open on his knee, needles stretched out in the air so as not to touch anything.

'What now?' asked Maria.

'According to the guidebook… insert the key where it looks important. On the right under the wheel. Then turn it.'

Maria inserted the key. Turned it. The engine rattled, the whole car jerked, the radio buzzed, and Maria nearly jumped out of her skin.

'Does it do that every time?!'

'Apparently,' muttered Martus. 'Quote: 'The backward roar of the engine signals the awakening of the vehicle. Do not be afraid. Usually.''

'Brilliant.'

Maria looked around, gripping the wheel like a lifeline.

'Where now?'

Martus flipped pages. 'Now grasp the gear lever. The D symbol means forward. Do not confuse it with R – that's probably a trap.'

'Alright.'

Maria put it in D. The car began to move slowly, creeping forward as though it were sizing them up. Maria started trembling, whiles Martus hissed quietly.

'Belts!'

'What?'

'Oh Deep! Safety belt. Strap yourself in. Otherwise humans will kill us, or at least fine us.'

Maria looked around. Found the belt. Got tangled in it like she'd been ambushed with ribbon in a kitchen.

They were moving for the first time, travelling as Deepers in a car on their way to find their prince. Martus kept his eyes on the road, reading as he went with quiet focus. 'If someone overtakes you and has their eyebrows joined into one line, move aside. Those are… taxi drivers.'

'Looks like I'll survive,' grumbled Maria.

'They said the same thing in the chapter on slugs. And then you limped for three days.'

The car turned. Maria grinned. Martus held onto the seat to avoid falling. Then a blue light flashed. Martus looked up.

'Blue light… that means it's the police.'

'Oh.'

'Pull over.'

Slamming the brake, Maria brought the car to a stop that was sharper than it should have been. Martus nearly stabbed the dashboard. The rear mirror showed a policeman approaching.

'Martus?' whispered Maria.

'Yes?'

'Can I keep him? For the wall?'

'No. Humans only get hung up when... never mind. Be polite.'

The policeman reached the window.

'Do you know you're driving five kilometres an hour?' he asked.

Maria looked at him with honest eyes, eyes that had witnessed the lives of kettles but had never seen a radar.

'Really? So I should slow down?'

The policeman hesitated. 'Slow down? No. The opposite, actually.'

'But...' Maria wavered. 'I was afraid that if I went too fast, the ground under the wheels would break.'

Martus leaned across her with the guidebook open, his thumb wedged between the pages. His needles clicked lightly, a sound he made when he was deep in thought or when he felt the urge to stab someone.

'In chapter sixteen it clearly states that the vehicle is a machine of both speed and death. It also says the steering wheel is not a dough ring from a bakery, which I must remind Maria.'

Maria hissed at him. 'I thought it was like a mixing bowl. Just bigger.'

The policeman narrowed his eyes. 'Do you... have a driving licence?'

'I don't know,' said Maria. 'But I've got a wooden spoon.'

'Are you joking? Were you drinking? Please, can you get out of the car?'

'But I can do more things with it than with this car.'

Martus shrugged. 'It's not written anywhere that a spoon is insufficient.'

The policeman inhaled. And then in the distance there was a sound: VVVVRRRMMM! A black car shot past. Noise like from another galaxy. The policeman turned, cursed, and ran towards it.

'Stay where you are! And for god's sake, don't park on the pavement!'

Maria looked at Martus.

'That was the pavement?'

Martus flipped through pages. 'Yes. Seems so.'

'Oh.'

They both leaned back. The engine still running. Maria was still gripping the wheel with both hands, holding it firm as if it might bite at any moment.

Martus let out a sigh. 'He said to wait, but for what? Are we still far?'

Maria kept her eyes on the road.

'We just go straight, right?'

'Unless we crash into a lamp-post, yes.'

And off they went again. At a slow five-kilometre speed. Dignified. Like ambassadors from a completely different world. Which they absolutely were.

They arrived to find the front of the studio looking like a pop star fan meet-up. There were posters and glowing banners with slogans like 'RODDY 4EVER', people wearing T-shirts with his face on them, and one man even had his silhouette tattooed on his calf.

Maria stopped and gasped.

'This is... He's got more fans than mine little pastries, Martus.'

'That's because pastries aren't magical plastic figurines with blinking eyes,' grumbled Martus, scowling around.

When they tried to get closer, security stopped them immediately. A tall gentleman with arms wide enough to hug a tree.

'No entry for the public. Staff only.'

'Errm... We're a team,' said Maria.

'Team of who?'

Martus opened his mouth, hesitated, then said, 'We're... the pastry team. Um... catering.'

Maria turned to him with a look that in the Deep would've triggered an explosion.

'Really? That's what you came up with?'

The guard frowned. 'Can I see your ID?'

Martus quickly pulled out the guidebook and flipped through it. 'Hm... Chapter 11: Grand entrances and subtle lies. 'If you want to pass unnoticed, act confident and never mention catering.''

'There it is then,' sighed Maria.

While the guard radioed in, Martus grabbed Maria's hand and pulled her aside.

'We need to find another way.'

They found a side door by the kitchen delivery entrance. Maria promptly nicked an apron from a nearby trolley and threw it over her Deeper apron.

'You look good,' said Martus.

'Thanks. I look like a walking tablecloth.'

'But a nice tablecloth.'

Maria blushed.

Martus shoved a paper hat on his head, something between a French baker and a sailor. His needles gleamed. They went in, walking past a table of cupcake trays, when a woman in a business suit appeared. She stopped and stared at Martus.

'You... you're from the agency?'

'Erm... yes?'

'Unbelievable! Your hands! Is that a costume?'

Martus looked at his needles. Then at her.

'Something like that.'

The woman laughed. 'Brilliant! You're an artist! We've just had a spot open in the design workshop. Want to give it a go?'

Maria pushed her aside. 'Excuse us, we're on a schedule!'

Martus just raised an eyebrow and smirked.

'Strategic pastries, right?'

Maria rolled her eyes and growled, 'Shut up and find Roddy.'

Martus stopped by a wall and peeked around the corner. One corridor, two doors, and one technician with a headset and a tablet. Next to him stood a cart of props. And in between was a chance. He looked back, but Maria was gone. Her apron fluttered and the cupcakes wobbled as she slipped confidently into the crowd, as though she understood human chaos.

He didn't understand it, but he admired it. The guidebook rustled in his pocket as he pulled it out. Chapter 14: How to get through when no one wants you to. 'Sometimes you don't need a plan. Sometimes all you need is hands like weapons and a look that says you know exactly where you're going.' He shut it. Slowly, with theatrical calm, he took his first step. The technician looked up.

'Oi! You—'

Martus raised his hand with the needles, not in a threatening way, but with elegance.

'Where's the main cast dressing room?' he said in the voice they used to issue orders in the Deep.

The technician swallowed, pointed. Martus nodded, walked past and tapped the technician's shoulder with one needle as he went, just enough to leave a little thread on his jumper. As the corridor widened, the sounds around him grew louder and the lights became harsher. He had the distinct sense that he was close.

Ahead of him hung a dark, heavy curtain, which Martus gently pulled aside. Beyond it, illuminated by the harsh glare of the stage lights, sat Roddy. He was positioned on a small pedestal, surrounded by cameras, crew, and people who looked as though they belonged in toothpaste adverts.

The figurine was small and shiny, yet unmistakably alive. His eyes blinked. Martus stepped forward, then took another step. Roddy froze. The movement was slight, almost imperceptible, but Martus saw it and understood. He was close now, still hidden, only a few metres away. And very soon, everything would change.

Meanwhile, outside, I stood at the edge of the madness. It felt like a carnival, but one without any real purpose. There were people everywhere, with stage music pounding through the air, flashing signs, and banners bearing the name RODDY. Some of them even sparkled. One bloke had the figurine's face tattooed on his leg. Yeah. Like, permanently. Probably.

'What is this madness?' I muttered, staring at the crowd.

Lucy laughed. 'This is television, sweetheart. People love a show., and Roddy's gone viral.'

'Viral...' I repeated the word like it burned. 'Sounds like an illness.'

'Sometimes it ends up that way,' she winked, tugging my sleeve.

We got closer. Security everywhere. Barriers. Cameras.

'How do we get in?' I asked.

Of course, Lucy had a plan. She always had a plan. She even had a plan for when to shove me aside, so I'd look less suspicious.

'Well, you're a boy. You've got a face. We'll make you a fan.'

'Sorry... of what?'

'Silent power, radiate interest, and maintain eye contact. It helps.'

Then she shoved a cap onto my head, one with a heart and the hashtag RoddyRules embroidered on it.

'I'll only take this off dead,' I muttered.

'Exactly what you want to say in a crowd,' Lucy said, already pulling me towards a side entrance for audience members. She moved quickly, weaving through the chaos as if she belonged there. Maybe I had that look, the kind that made people assume I knew what I was doing. It seemed to help, and for once, I was glad of it.

Chapter Twenty-Five
The Strength

We slipped inside just as the show began. The air changed, filled with heat and noise. Lights flashed across the walls. Music pulsed through the space, and ahead, beneath the stage lights, stood Roddy. He was on a platform, glowing faintly, small and still, smiling like the moment had been made for him.

I stopped, unsure of what I was seeing. At first, the stage was too bright, the details too sharp, too stylised. It felt like something from a dream stitched out of cheap television and old posters. But then I noticed the hands. They moved with quiet precision, thin fingers tipped with needles catching the light. I recognised them. Beside Roddy stood a man, holding a suit clearly tailored for someone of Roddy's size. He was adjusting the collar, calm and focused, as though preparing something important. Something sacred. I blinked.

It was Martus. A tight breath caught in my chest. My grip closed around the railing beside me. He stood on a stage, in the human world, among cameras and strangers. He had crossed over. And nothing about it made sense.

'That's Martus,' I said, my voice low.

Lucy leaned forward. 'The one with the needles?'

I nodded.

'Then that is actually pretty cool,' she said.

I wanted to agree, but I couldn't. My mind was scrambling. He shouldn't be here. He wasn't supposed to be here. I had no idea how he had come, or why, or what he was even doing. There had been no warning, no sign, nothing. Martus didn't belong on a stage in the human world, standing beside a talking figurine in front of lights and cameras. The whole thing felt unreal, like I was watching a dream slip sideways into something else.

I stared, trying to find sense in it, but none came. We watched as he adjusted Roddy's collar with quiet care. His face was unreadable, but I recognised the focus in his movements. Then, slowly, he looked up and met my eyes. There was a single blink, followed by the slight lift of one eyebrow. The same look he used to give me when I had done something wrong. When I had made a mess and didn't know it yet.

Something shifted in me. A strange mix of confusion, unease, and something I could only call fear. I had no idea what was happening. But I knew, without question, that everything was about to change.

Right then the presenter shouted something about 'a special moment with our design genius!' and the crowd exploded in applause. Martus shrugged, as if to say what can you do, and bowed. At first, it looked like a glitch. Roddy froze. His body, once a polished plastic figurine about the size of a Ken doll, became completely still. His head tilted slightly to one side, arms falling to his sides in a way that seemed too controlled to be accidental.

Then came a sound. It was not mechanical but deeper, as though something internal had finally clicked into place. His eyes blinked. It was not animation, and it was not caused by LEDs. It was light, sharp, white, and unwavering, and it came from somewhere real.

That was the moment it began. From the centre of Roddy's palm, something narrow began to slide out. At first it looked like a needle, but as it extended, it became clear that it was more like a nozzle.

It was made of black metal and barely visible unless it moved. Even then, it only caught the light in quick, shifting glimpses. Roddy lifted his arm and pointed it at the front row of the crowd. Light broke over the room. It had the look of a camera flash, yet the air stayed mute, no click or hum to explain it. The glare caught on a fifteen-year-old girl wearing a T-shirt printed with *Roddy is life*.

Her reaction was not what anyone might have expected. She did not scream or fall. Her entire body simply stopped. Her arms lowered. Her face became completely expressionless. Her eyes remained open, but the life behind them vanished. It looked as though something inside her had been quietly closed, like curtains being drawn in a room that had suddenly gone still. A soft blue mark began to glow on her forehead. It was a symbol I recognised immediately, a mark used in Deep-level tech. I had seen it before, too many times to count. It meant that a process had begun.

There was no outward change to her body, no physical transformation, at least not yet. But something internal had been activated. The signal had been received, and now the mechanism was quietly ticking forward inside her.

Roddy moved his hand again and turned slightly to face the next target. Another flash appeared, identical to the first. This time the light struck a teenage boy in a dark hoodie. He collapsed briefly onto one knee as if his body had lost control, but within seconds he stood upright again. His face was slack and unreadable.

When he opened his eyes, the change was unmistakable. They had lost all trace of human detail. There were no pupils, just a smooth, uniform grey that gave no sense of depth or awareness. The same pattern continued. More flashes followed. One after the other, they passed through the crowd in clean, deliberate rhythm. Each beam struck a new person. Each result was the same.

People stopped moving. They either fell to the ground or froze in place. The effect was quiet and exact. Roddy's movements were neither rushed nor hesitant. He was operating with the calm precision of something executing a programmed task.

At first, the audience responded as though it were all part of the show. Some laughed, thinking it was a clever lighting trick. Others clapped, still expecting a reveal or explanation. That illusion did not last long. Once a handful of people collapsed without moving, once their eyes opened and showed only grey, the tension in the room shifted. Someone screamed.

A woman pushed through the crowd and tripped over a seat. Another man stumbled into a barrier while trying to turn around. The panic did not come all at once. It spread slowly, step by step, as more people began to realise that what they were seeing was not staged. A young girl started crying. The man beside her reached out to help but suddenly stopped and stared at nothing.

People screamed. Others tried to run but were blocked by those who remained frozen in place. They stood upright, unmoving, their eyes empty. Their bodies looked perfectly fine, but whatever was inside them had changed. They no longer looked like audience members. They looked like replicas of him, each one standing still with the same vacant expression.

He moved through the centre of the stage, surrounded by fog, lights, and smoke. There was no pause in his motion and no suggestion of dance or performance. Every step followed a steady, measured rhythm, as if he were carrying out a task far beyond human understanding. Every gesture followed a smooth, mechanical rhythm. There was no emotion in his steps, no sense of joy or fear. He seemed to be shifting from one internal mode to another, as if his entire structure was recalibrating in real time.

Lucy turned to me and spoke, her voice quiet and broken. She said it as if she were trying to convince herself it wasn't true.

'This can't be real.'

I did not answer her. I could not. Because I knew exactly what I was seeing, and I had seen it before. Years ago, I had stood in a Deep lab and watched a demonstration that never should have happened.

Back then, my father still lived at home, and Roddy's function had been nothing more than an idea, an experiment that had been locked away for good reason. That function had been shut down. Deemed too dangerous. It was never supposed to exist outside a sealed testing chamber. It was never meant to be activated. And yet, here it was. Someone had restored it.

Roddy was no longer a showpiece or a harmless creation. He was carrying out the instructions he had once been built to follow. Minds bent to him, not through violence, but with a quiet, seamless surrender. What he performed was more than control. It was a rewrite that began deep inside and worked its way outward.

He was no longer simply part of the world we recognised. The boundaries had shifted, and with every silent flash, he reshaped what it meant to be human.

My body moved before the decision had even formed. Thoughts lagged behind, but my feet were already crossing the floor. The stage swam in light and thick smoke. Security lined its edges in black, masked faces turning them into creatures rather than guards. None of that held me. My gaze was fixed only on him.

Roddy stood in the centre of the chaos, calm and still, the source of everything that had gone wrong. Even though everything I had just witnessed, I saw more than the weapon he had become.

I saw my friend. Something deep inside me, far past fear or reason, clung to the idea that I could still bring him back. The thought pulled me forward and I leapt the barrier. Lucy came after me. Around us people screamed; someone was sick in the corner; others pushed the other way. None of it touched me. All that mattered was one thought repeating in my head. Get to him.

Security spotted us. Two moved. One from the left, one from the right. The first went straight for Lucy – she knocked him out with her handbag before he could say 'hey'. The second came for me. I felt my heart pounding. My body moved on its own. Slipped past him, spun, sprinted for the stage. A needle flew past my head – Roddy had seen me. But he did not stop. Jumping over the ramp, I slipped on a cable and nearly lost my footing, but my hand shot forward and caught him.

He slid into my grip just as he always had. His body remained rigid, eyes still glowing faintly, but something in the contact changed. For a moment, he responded. It was brief, but I felt it. Then came a click from deep inside him. The lights went out. A loud bang echoed from somewhere at the back of the stage. It could have been an explosion, or just a light falling. Either way, it didn't matter.

Lucy's hand found mine, and together we ran. We tore through the dressing rooms and into a maze of white corridors, not stopping to look behind. And there they were, by the loos.

Martus and Maria.

She was holding a tray of pastries like she had personally sworn to protect them from the apocalypse. Martus stood beside her, wild-eyed, like someone who had just seen a ghost do something inappropriate.

'Tonny?' they both said in unison.

'Martus? Maria? What in the Deep are you doing here?' My voice came out in a breathless wheeze.

Maria looked like she was about to burst into tears, but instead she launched herself at me, nearly flattening Roddy in the process. She hugged me so tightly I thought she might snap my ribs, tray of pastries still perfectly balanced in one hand.

Martus had a single tear in his eye. Just one. Tastefully placed. Almost cinematic.

'We came to save you, my pie,' Maria said, sniffling. 'And look at you, you've lost weight. I could fold you in a drawer.'

Any hope of answering vanished as someone shouted behind us. Heavy footsteps were heading our way, fast.

'Right,' I said. 'Touching reunion. Emotional pastries. Very moving. But we really have to run.'

The corridor lights flickered. Doors at the far end slammed open with dramatic timing. An alarm blared overhead. The intercom crackled to life with the cheerful message, 'Security protocol two. Everyone to their positions.' By then, we were already legging it.

Lucy jammed the key into the lock of a very stolen-looking car. We all piled in with the grace of a collapsing wardrobe. I slid into the back seat, clutching Roddy on my lap. He was still frozen, but definitely still present. If he blinked, I was ready.

The engine coughed, groaned, and then roared like it had just remembered it was supposed to be heroic. And we drove straight into the dark.

'So what now?' Martus asked, casually flicking one of his needles just as I looked away from Lucy.

'We need to get back to the Deep,' I said. 'Quickly. I just have no idea how.'

Roddy stirred.

'I can take us back,' he said quietly. 'But I'm not sure it'll work. I'm almost out of strength.'

'Try, Roddy,' I said.

Maria and Martus didn't argue. Lucy glanced at me, then looked forward again.

'Maybe you should pull over, Lucy,' I said. And she did.

No one moved. Not even Roddy. Then something changed. The pressure didn't burst outward. It pulled inward, as if something had been released. Roddy shifted at my side, his head tilting, his small hands rising, and I realised with a jolt that they were not mine.

They were his. Real. Too small for the task. He pressed his palms together, then gave them a little shake, like someone getting ready to jump into cold water. The space in front of him changed. It was as though the air had opened right in front of us. We stepped out.

A thin opening appeared, only just wide enough to notice if you already knew it was there.

'Hold on tight, everyone. It will be fast,' Roddy said. And we all held hands. I grabbed Lucy's, Lucy Maria's and Martus Maria's second hand. I was ready, we all were, but nothing happened. We all looked at each other, confused.

'Roddy? What now?' I said.

He stayed quiet. Suddenly, everything started to change, slowly disappearing: the roads, the cars, the grass and even the trees around us. But I didn't feel the movement. Then the smell came. First metal, then something stale, the kind of dry tang you get from old machines. It seemed heavy, as though it had travelled far to reach us. Underneath it all was a colder trace, one I knew too well. The Deep.

Maria's face was grey. Martus was struggling to breathe. Lucy held Roddy up. Her hands were shaking from effort. The opening held, and we went through. No one hesitated.

I stepped first.

As soon as I crossed, I felt it. Not like a wave, but more like a door finally opening. The air on the other side knew me. It didn't feel good, but it felt right. I could breathe again. The air here didn't weigh me down. It grounded me. Maria laughed. She ran in a circle, kicking up the red dust. Martus stood still and breathed deeply, like it was the first time in days. Lucy spun on the spot and looked up.

'This looks like something Tim Burton would design if he went on holiday,' she said.

I didn't reply. I crouched and touched the ground. Cold stone. Familiar. I didn't need to remember it. My body already knew it.

'We're home,' I said.

No one disagreed. The hug came naturally. Martus looked surprised, then stood straighter. Maria hugged Lucy. Lucy hugged me. Roddy moved quietly in my pocket. Feeling that everything was all right hadn't happened in days.

Something shifted. Heavy with warning, a sound followed. They stepped out from behind the pillars. Human in body, wrong in movement, empty where faces should have been. Behind them stood Alan. His hands were behind his back. His head was tilted. He looked relaxed. Like this wasn't strange at all. He smiled with a calm that lacked both warmth and arrogance, and that was what made it harder to bear.

'Welcome home,' he said.

His words felt heavy. They landed and stayed. I looked around. Something was wrong. We were in the Deep. But it wasn't like before. It was darker. Heavier was the silence. The stairs looked unstable, like they might shift when you weren't watching.

'What is going on here?' I asked.

Searching for a voice, I turned, only to be met by the pressure of silence. The three of them stood behind me, pale, rigid, their attention locked on Alan. They did not move, yet I felt their fear like a current through the room.

With quiet steps, Alan moved forward, staring at Lucy. He said nothing, only came closer until he was near enough to breathe her in. A long, clear breath filled the space. Lucy froze, her jaw clenched, and for a moment she held still. Then she edged back, wiping at her arm as though the act could strip away what had just happened. Alan smiled.

'Ah. Human. You brought a human into the Deep. That's forbidden. You know that, don't you?'

Lucy didn't reply. She kept her eyes on him. Maria moved closer to me. Her breathing was light. Martus stayed still, but I could see the tension in his shoulders. His needles shook slightly. Alan looked at all of us.

'All of you will pay for your wickedness,' he said.

Then he looked at me.

'The Prince of the Deep,' he said. 'Gone.'

Toward him, I took a step.

'What do you mean, gone? I'm right here. I'm—'

I never finished. As Alan lifted his hand, the room had already begun to shift. He didn't need to shout or move quickly; his fingers opened and the space obeyed. Nothing moved, nothing spoke, but the air pressed in tight as though the room itself was shrinking. Falling and any sense of motion were both absent. One moment we stood in the hall; the next we were inside a cell.

Chapter Twenty-six

The Bars

'Tonny? Is that you?!' asked Maria, or more accurately, shouted.

I got up from the cold floor and placed my hand on the wall.

'I'm here,' I said.

There was a muffled thud from a different direction. It came from the cell next to mine. That was definitely Martus. He didn't say anything, but I knew it was him. Whenever he banged or made noise, he used his elbow. Instantly, I knew what it was. Smiling, I felt a weight lift from my chest when I realised they were all alright. Even if we were locked up and kind of screwed, at least we were together. And alive.

I sat down in the corner. The darkness around me wasn't the dramatic kind, you know? More like worn out. Stone walls. A bit of cold air. In the Deep, things don't decay, but even so, it smelt like the end. From the next cell came the sound of a soft hiccup. Then another.

Closing my eyes was all I did.

'Martus... I just... I can't breathe,' whispered Maria, sounding like steam escaping from a kettle.

'Then don't breathe,' growled Martus, but it wasn't cruel. That was just how he was. It was like offering you a blanket by smacking you with it.

'I... I just... maybe you could use your needles instead of all that banging and not be so grumpy.'

'Needles? And what am I supposed to do with those? Sew you a blanket?'

Maria sniffed. 'You're absolutely useless.'

'Enough, you two,' I said, and sighed. 'I'm the useless one. It's all my fault.'

'Erm... you kind of forgot about me. I'm here too. I think I'm in the cell next to Maria. I can hear everything,' came Lucy's voice.

Because I didn't want to show emotion, I inhaled deeply.

'Are you alright?' asked Maria, as though she were pulling the sentence out of that secret drawer where you keep the things you're scared to say aloud.

'No,' said Martus.

'Nobody asked you!' Maria shouted.

'There's no toilet,' said Lucy, and there was a hint of shame in her voice. I understood, of course. In the Deep, no one really peed. The toilets and plumbing had been installed for me, not for the prisoners.

'Good luck. No peeing here,' said Martus.

I closed my eyes and leaned against the wall.

'I'm sorry, Lucy… for everything.'

No one replied, and the room stayed quiet. Trying not to move, I lowered my head, and told myself it was time to stop feeling sorry. I had to grow up, stop complaining, and actually do something. I was the Prince of the Deep, and I should never have let it come to this. Maybe it was already too late, but there was still a chance to repair what I could.

I tried to piece together a plan. That was when I heard something. Soft footsteps. Slow, even, like they were being timed. Steps of that sort could only be those of one individual.

Alan, of course.

He appeared between our cells, calm as always. His hands were behind his back, and his face was unreadable. Then he snapped his fingers. The walls of our cells changed into iron bars. Now we could all see each other.

Maria was lying on the floor, eating biscuits from her apron. Martus was leaning against the wall. Lucy was pacing like she needed the toilet. They all stepped closer. Standing in the centre, Alan acted as if we were supposed to bow, and we all watched.

'I hoped you were feeling better,' he said to Lucy. His tone was polite, but something felt off.

I didn't answer. I just looked at him.

He slowly turned to face me and gave a small familiar wink. Like he knew me too well.

'Your father would be proud,' he said. 'And you know that.'

'Where is he?' I asked. My voice was low but firm.

'Alive,' he said.

I breathed in. Moving a little closer, I approached the bars. He leaned in slightly, and what he said next was meant only for me.

'I hated him. More than I ever hated you. Which, yes, I know is hard to believe.'

I blinked.

'What?'

'Yes. Your father. Death. The great and mighty ruler. But do you know what no one ever saw? How cruel he really was. How cold. In truth, he doesn't even have a heart.'

He smiled, and I told myself not to react, only to hope he wouldn't launch into some long, dramatic story about how hard his life had been. Of course he did.

After letting out a sigh, I lowered my head.

'Your father made me,' he said. 'Shaped me to serve him. But I'm not some tool. He treated me like dirt. Made me polish his boots. And... I had to look after you too!'

He started pacing.

'But Alfonzo was different. You see... with him I mattered, I was worth something, and he never once made me clean his boots.'

'My grandfather?' I said.

'Yes. You were blind, and worse, you were stupid,' he said. 'This is all mine now. I'm the one in charge, you silly, fool... you're nothing. I guess, now you can polish my boots, or maybe... Lucy can.'

I froze. I could feel the hatred coming off him. It was real. Now I understood his excessive talking. He needed to let it out.

'You'll pay for this!'

Alan didn't reply. He smiled again.

'Come closer. I'll stitch needles into your face. Might make you look better!' Martus shouted.

Maria held up her wooden spoon like a weapon.

Alan laughed.

'Fools. This is exactly why Alfonzo picked me. Because all of you are useless. But that's going to change. The Deep will change. Under my rule, no one will stand above me. I'll build an army. The Deep will take control. I will become Death.'

At that I couldn't help myself and laughed, because the whole thing had tipped into comedy, and soon enough the others were laughing too. Alan frowned and looked around, first at Maria, then Martus, then Lucy, and finally at me.

'I had planned to kill you with… less pain. But now I'll need a new plan. One that hurts.'

I told myself the same thing again. The Prince of the Deep, blind all the same. It should have been clear. To believe Alan, the quiet man in the suit, was foolish. To believe my grandfather was only helping for a while, that he would step aside once my father returned, was worse.

With my eyes closed the memories came one after another. My grandfather at the council. The way he made me stand. The way he sat down, as if the throne had always belonged to him. Now, the reason for it was plain.

He had never been protecting me. Believing he was had been my mistake. Alan had only ever been part of the plan, nothing more. I buried my fingers in my hair. It didn't hurt physically, but it hit somewhere deeper. That part where you hide the feelings you don't want to deal with. And now there was nowhere left to put them.

Lucy's eyes were on me. She kept quiet, and that was the worst part. Words would have given me something to push against, something to answer or argue, but her silence left no doubt that I had messed it all up.

I held my tongue. It was at that moment that I first considered I might not be as intelligent as I fancied myself.

A sound shifted in front of me.

'Did you hear that?' Martus whispered.

'Of course I did. I've got ears,' said Maria. 'And a heart. And it's telling me our dear prince has just decided to give up.'

'I wasn't talking to you, Maria. I was talking to Tonny,' Martus said.

Maria opened her mouth to reply, but I spoke first.

'I'm not giving up. I am the Prince of the Deep. I'm the guardian and the rightful heir to the throne.'

'Finally,' said Lucy. 'Which is exactly why you need to lift that royal backside of yours, got it?'

She probably still needed the toilet.

I looked up. Maria was holding something that looked like a rock-hard pastry and pointing it at the door.

'Maria, that's not a grenade,' Martus muttered.

'And how do you know?' she replied.

'Because I'm bloody sure, that's how,' he said.

They fell quiet, but they didn't stop looking at me. I didn't like the way they were looking. Like they still believed in me. Like I still deserved it.

Then we heard a soft click.

My cell door opened at a slow pace. It was so quiet, it took a second to realise what was happening. I turned my head.

One of the Guardians of the Deep stood there. He wore a dark suit. The symbol of Death was on his collar. A ring of keys hung from his hand.

Those eyes were not Alan's and not my grandfather's either. What I saw in them was gentleness, a trace of sorrow, and a certainty that could not be doubted.

'Prince,' he said. 'Your father meant everything to me. And you are his blood.' He reached out his hand. 'Let me help. And forgive us for leaving you in here. It wasn't our choice. Alan is holding us. He's already killed several of our own.'

'Killed?' I asked.

'He sent the Dustdreads. If we refuse to obey, we disappear.'

My chest felt tight. But I reached out and placed my hand in his.

'I'll fix it. Don't worry,' I said.

'I know.'

And that meant something. It showed he believed me, that he still had faith. What I needed most was to know my people had not lost their trust, and to believe I could give them something in return.

'Now go. Act like nothing happened,' I told him.

After nodding, he walked away. On his face was the quiet imprint: I believe in you.

Then I unlocked the others' cells. Maria was chewing something that looked like baked stone. Martus was winding thread around his wrist, like he always did when he was thinking. Lucy looked like her bladder was about to burst.

'Go over there. Upstairs. First right. Just… be quiet and fast… make sure no one sees you,' I told her, and Lucy ran.

'So,' I said to Maria and Marus. 'We need to split up.'

Maria raised an eyebrow. 'Deeps love… That line always comes just before everyone dies.'

'Yes, in fairy tales. In the Deep it just means half of us are going to get slapped harder,' said Martus.

Maria swallowed. 'I want to go with you,' she said to me.

'So do I,' growled Martus.

'You two will go together,' I told them.

'I don't want to,' said Martus.

'Can you both stop acting like children? This really is not the time for it,' I snapped.

They looked at each other. And smiled. I just hoped it wasn't one of those fake smiles. Lucy came back.

'No one saw you?' I asked. She shook her head. 'Good.'

'So, you two,' I pointed at Maria and Martus, 'you'll go after Alan. We know he's taken over, but he still doesn't have full power. Somewhere, there's a weakness. And who else is going to find it if not...' I glanced at Martus, 'Mr Needle and Miss Pastry.'

'Say that again and I'll sew you pyjamas out of spider venom,' hissed Martus.

'Deal.'

Lucy folded her arms. 'And us?'

I looked at her.

'We're going after my grandfather.'

'That sounds... worse than going after Alan,' Lucy said.

'I know.'

I stood up. So did the others.

'When you're with Alan, don't kill him right away,' I said. 'I want to know where my dad is.'

Maria nodded. Martus shrugged.

'We'll see what's left of him.'

Lucy handed me a small plum pastry from her pocket. I had no idea how long it had been in there.

'For luck,' she said.

I remembered how that first plum tasted in her car. And that moment when everything had still been simple. Well… sort of. The air tensed. It was like before a storm. Only this time, *we* were the storm.

Chapter Twenty-seven
Deepers

The concrete was gone. Dark, aged stone was beneath them. Each step showed it held memory, more than weather or footsteps, something deeper. Maria shifted. Martus kept his hands close. The surrounding walls were tall and disappeared into the darkness above. It was not an empty silence but one crowded by something unseen. The stone shone with gentle lines, the hum in the air giving the room the pull of memory.

Maria held her stained apron. Her fingers gripped it tightly. Martus walked next to her without speaking. His body was tense. Signs and superstitions meant nothing to him, but he was watching closely, sensing there was more underneath and refusing to let it surprise him.

'Wow,' Maria said after a few steps.

'I know,' Martus answered without turning, his eyes fixed on her.

A man stepped from a side corridor, neither rushing nor hiding, as if he knew it was not his moment. Wearing a cloak and an eye covering, he looked older, but he still stood with dignity. At Martus's sight his face eased, unusual for a Deeper.

'Martus,' he said. The name came slowly, like it had been pulled out from somewhere buried. 'My best student.'

Martus frowned, though it was habit more than rejection. He always hid behind walls when he lacked an answer. As the man came closer, he raised a needle and touched it to the man's back. The purpose was not to drive him away, but instead to give a careful embrace.

Still, Maria did not budge. Her breath was held, not with fear but with something rising inside her. It showed in her eyes, and then a tear ran down her cheek. She let it fall.

More shapes came from the corridors, moving without words or haste. They stepped out until the walls lost their emptiness. The Deepers came slowly, one by one. No two were alike. Some had skin like cracked glass. Others like polished stone. Their eyes didn't look like strangers'. When they saw Maria and Martus, they stopped. As if something they had waited for had finally returned.

A voice rose from the crowd, tight with emotion. 'He's back. Martus. And the kitchen girl.'

Shifting her weight, Maria lifted her shoulders.

'Cook,' she said clearly. The small smile that followed was for herself, not anyone else. That word mattered.

The smile faded, leaving calm. The silence grew, not still but restless as the air shifted and the light thickened above. Threads from the lamps shook. Dust moved. Some dragging, some striking hard, the footsteps followed, uneven but steady. Voices came after, faint and unclear, only bits of names and phrases from the Deep.

They meant nothing, yet they felt known. Alan stood on the balcony, hands on the rail, standing straight, eyes cold. As the sound rose, the corners of his mouth moved and his control slipped. His eyes no longer held steady. 'What is this?' he asked the room. He did not get to say more.

A quiet release sounded as the doors beneath the balcony opened. Martus stepped through, calm and steady, his presence natural. Maria came with him, her clothes old, her stare firm, her hands folded in her apron.

Behind them came the others. Deepers who had gone unseen for years. One carried a ladle. Another hummed a tune no one knew. Like a flag, someone waved a cloth bearing a pastry image of a glazed sweet roll.

Backing away, Alan moved.

'This is not your place,' he said. His voice grew louder, sharper. 'You're servants, you are—'

'We are the Deepers!' Maria said.

Repeating the words was what the others did. Martus lifted his hand, the needles catching the light, and at once the room fell quiet.

'The strange thing is,' he said, his voice quiet but strong, 'none of us has power. And yet, you're the one who cannot leave.'

His eyes widened, and he turned. There was no passage through the corridors. Figures stood there now: old staff, faces long forgotten, Deepers he had stopped seeing.

'We want Death back,' someone called. Then others joined. Not shouting. Just speaking with intent.

'We want the family back.'

Martus nodded, and three Deepers stepped forward. Calmly, they moved, without any indication of fear or haste. Alan was neither dragged nor tied, and he offered no resistance. Maria walked after them.

Before he disappeared, she leaned down and said, 'That's for Tonny.' Her voice was steady.

No answer came from Alan.

With the soft certainty of a decision, the door closed behind him. No one clapped, yet the silence felt lighter. Alan sat in his cell and remained quiet, not from emptiness but because no one wished to listen.

Martus kept his gaze away. Maria offered no words. Deepers passed without turning. The stillness carried the weight of an ending. Not as an act of revenge, but because the choice was final, the door closed.

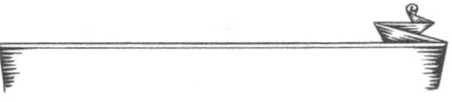

Chapter Twenty-eight
Fabric Snakes

The Deep had no roads. There were ribbons. Huge, rustling, self-moving strips of fabric that floated through the air like snakes. Travellers jumped on them (sometimes it was like riding a cobra) and let themselves be carried. Each ribbon had its own 'route memory'; it remembered where it usually went.

Bonus: If someone rode for the first time, the ribbon tested them. It checked whether they were 'of the Deep' or not. Depending on the answer, it either settled or shook them off.

When I said ribbons, I didn't mean the kind you tie round a birthday present. I meant wide streams of fabric that hovered over the ground like centipedes without legs. Each one had a colour. Each one rustled. And each lived a life of its own.

Standing at the edge of a cliff was where we stopped. Below me, four ribbons rolled and shimmered: dark green, blue, grey, and the last one…

gold. Gold in the Deep never shone; it breathed. This one breathed slowly. It was waiting.

Lucy stood still, watching the fabric twist and move on its own, saw that there was no structure underneath, no logic. Just air and flowing.

'That's... that's transport?' she asked slowly.

'Yeah. Snakes. Fabric snakes. They take you anywhere. You just have to know where you want to go.'

She stepped closer.

'And how do you... like... get on?'

I smirked. 'Exactly how you think.'

'You're joking.'

'Nope. You just run and jump.'

'You jump on... a conscious scarf snake?'

'Yeah. With memory.'

'...God.'

'Don't bother, he's got dementia, poor thing... anyway, we're not very creative with names in the Deep, but the system structure's solid.'

Lucy gave me a look that said: if this thing eats me, I swear I'll haunt you after death.

Kneeling, she touched the ribbon's edge, and it purred.

She blinked.

'Did it... strike me? Or I stroked it?'

'It's testing you.'

'Testing what?'

'If you're from here. If it should carry you... or throw you off.'

'What?!'

'Don't worry. With me, you'll be fine.'

I held out my hand. She grabbed it tight, and as we ran, I could feel her heart start pounding. Then... we jumped. The ribbon caught us without hesitation. The first few seconds were like a water slide. Then it turned into gliding, swimming through the air, corners, waves, pressure, and then... weightlessness. Lucy screamed, not in fear, but like someone who had just realised that rules didn't apply. 'THIS IS LIKE SURFING ON LSD!' she shouted in my ear.

'I DON'T KNOW WHAT THAT IS!' I shouted back.

'IT'S A COMPLIMENT!'

I smiled. Really smiled.

The Deep rolled beneath us as the ribbon began to slow, not suddenly, but gradually, like the way you slow down when you grow tired of running. Then everything went quiet. Lucy was silent. So was I, not because there was nothing to say, more because I was looking at her. At how she looked around, at us, at the Deep. It was clear she liked it. Her face lit up so much that I even thought maybe she was prettier than

Amelia. Which couldn't be, because Amelia was meant to be the most beautiful. Meant to.

Below us, the Deep opened up, stretching out in every direction.

Because our sky was green, she looked at it, and it was not like grass, but more like what you see when an emerald shatters and is held up to the light. Lamps floated in the air, not hanging from anything, just drifting like fish. Some had eyes, real ones, and one of them even winked at me. I noticed, of course, but pretended I hadn't.

'Wow, this is beautiful...' she whispered, her mouth slightly open.

I smiled at her. I liked it. I really did.

It was the first time in ages I had respected the Deep. Home again. Once I had resisted coming back, and now I did not want to leave. A hand pointed down, giving her the chance to see for herself.

The houses... well, calling them houses was a stretch. One was made of fabric that was clearly not ordinary. Another seemed built from dust. Some shifted colour with mood, and one even had legs and ran off.

Lucy looked at it all, her mouth slightly open and head tilted. She didn't ask anything. Not yet. She probably didn't know where to begin.

'You alright?' I said.

'Erm... yeah... just... I didn't imagine the underworld would look like this, you know... I... I'm impressed,' she said.

'Yes, I had the same feeling about your human world.'

'It feels like I'm in a fairy tale. I feel like I'm going mad. Is this real?'

'Of course it's real,' I laughed.

We passed a market where they sold the things people lost in dreams, such as single gloves and lethal emeralds. Not at us, but at me, the Deepers then waved. In that moment, I straightened a little, not out of pride, but because it felt right, almost instinctive.

'They know who you are,' said Lucy.

I didn't reply, just nodded, because yes, I supposed they did; I was their prince.

The ribbon slid on, moving more slowly now, calmer and more certain.

Lucy looked at me differently. Not in that 'you've got something on your face' kind of way, but more like she finally saw me. Not the gentleman passing through, not the mess she had to drag along, but someone who actually belonged here. Maybe even someone who had brought her here, which, let's be honest, was the truth.

Something almost slipped out, a thought about telling her I liked looking at her. Her eyes had a flicker

I hadn't seen since the day we met. I didn't fully understand it, but it was there, a quiet joy as if she had remembered something good about the world.

A Deeper with a lantern for a head flew past us and beat its wings so hard that Lucy nearly toppled. I caught her, and somehow her hand ended up in mine. Without thinking I kept hold of it and didn't let go. She stayed still, her eyes resting on me.

I thought that even in a world completely off its rocker, there might still be something that made sense. I realised then she was more beautiful than Amelia, not just in the usual way, but in a way that was kinder, softer, and entirely different.

I wanted to kiss her. We were close, close enough to feel it. Her lips moved towards mine with deliberate slowness and caution because we both knew what was about to happen. The ribbon tugged. Not dramatically, not like in those films where everything spins wildly before crashing down. More like when someone steps into a lift, forgets to press a button, and just stands there waiting for the world to move. And in that awkward stillness, we saw them.

Dustdreads.

Oh yes. Them.

Not a few, not even a vague group in the distance. They were everywhere. Left, right, in front, behind.

Every place you would not want something slavering and semi-corporeal to be, they were.

Lucy pressed herself against me so quickly there was hardly time to catch a proper breath. Words felt pointless; what could be said while surrounded by creatures that looked ready to eat a person's spleen raw? Trying to stay calm, or at least give the impression of being calm, I held her close and focused on steady breaths.

Then something stirred inside me. But not panic, and not some noble sense of bravery. It felt more like that inner voice you usually ignore because it sounds too much like your disappointed aunt. Only this time, it said that I had to stop being tragic. I was a prince. Son of Death. These creatures were supposed to listen to me. And the terrifying part was that I actually believed it.

The ribbon began to slow down on its own. It was strange, because I had given no command, sent no mental signal, and whispered no sweet nothings into the air. It slowed, as if it had sensed something or already knew we had arrived. We hadn't, not yet. The change was because of them, and that was what struck me. Even so, I was not afraid.

Lucy was. She was shaking, clinging to me so tightly that my arm had gone numb. If it had not been such a horror show of a moment, I might have asked her to ease up. But I stayed quiet and let her hold on. When the Dustdreads came close enough for me to smell whatever chemical atrocity they were exhaling, something between rotting kelp and expired yoghurt, Lucy began to cry. Not loudly, but visibly… that hurt more than I had expected.

So I told her not to be scared. There was no heroic tone, just a quiet sentence offered because someone had to say something, and that someone, of course, was me.

Then one of the Dustdreads moved forward with deliberate steps, as though every movement was part of a ceremony I had not been invited to. I braced for something awful. Genuinely, I thought that was it. That he would lunge, or spit acid, or perform some horrific scream that turned us inside out.

But instead he leaned in, sniffed around me and said, 'My lord, forgive me.'

Forgive me? Lord?

Almost laughing, though it was a lie, I found my mind too busy reconfiguring to keep up with what had just happened.

'I don't understand,' I said.

'I can smell Death on you. You are our Lord, and we are waiting for your command,' he said.

As I looked at him, my heart changed, maybe even with pride.

'How can you smell Death? That is my father, not me. I can't command you.'

'No, my lord. We are Dustdreads. We are never wrong. We came from you; you made us; we carry you inside us. We can smell you, and now we are waiting for your command.'

'All right then, go back to where you came from. No more Dustdreads, all of you.'

After speaking, he stepped back. There was no nervousness in it, only space being made. He lifted one twisted limb, and every slimy, wheezing creature copied him. They withdrew together in perfect rhythm. Their steps struck like a heavy drumline, and in that sound I felt something new. Respect, not fear. And I liked it. No... I loved it.

Lucy stopped shaking and let go of me. The ribbon started moving again, slowly, as if it too had realised that something had shifted.

'How is this possible?'

'I do not know. He called me 'my lord',' I told her, trying to sound calm, maybe even a little unimpressed, though inside I was a cocktail of confusion and raw, rising certainty.

Something in them had recognised something in me. Maybe a trace of my father. Maybe the part of me I had ignored for too long. Maybe it was blood, lineage, some deeply buried inheritance that had decided to wake up. Real it was, whatever the thing was.

The ribbon picked up speed again. Purpose returned.

Lucy stayed silent, took my hand with quiet trust, and smiled. Pride or relief, I could not tell. Politics seemed pointless. The change, which melted my heart, was the most important thing.

Chapter Twenty-nine
Outside the Palace

When we landed, the ribbon gently touched the ground, with no jolt. Just a quiet brush, like it was saying goodbye. I jumped down first and helped Lucy. Of course, I was a gentleman. In front of us stood a palace. Nor was it a dark castle filled with skulls and flames. It was beautiful. Bright, smooth stone changed colour with the sky. At that moment, it was golden with a tint of violet as that strange Deep light set. They had slim, smooth columns. Without handles, the doors stood tall and silent, appearing to be waiting for someone's order.

'This is your grandfather...' Lucy did not even finish. She just stood there, staring.

'Yeah,' I answered.

'Brand new, isn't it?'

'Not really. He built it when he became Death. After Dad... after my father.'

Lucy looked around like someone who had just realised even the end could be beautiful. I focused. Standing at the door were guards. Two Deepers in suits made of woven mist. They looked calm, but their eyes watched everything.

'We will not get through that way,' I said quietly. 'We need to go around.'

If you walked too close, the hedge would whisper as we walked along the palace wall. Lucy glanced at it and pulled her hoodie tighter. We found a recess, almost like a terrace, only without access. Perhaps it had once been for servants, or a secret way out long ago. We hid behind the corner, in the shadows.

Lucy leaned in. 'You got a plan?'

I looked at her face, her eyes from the human world, and yet no longer quite belonging there.

'Not really,' I said. 'But this is not a family reunion anymore.'

'Is this war?' she asked.

'No,' I smiled. 'This is coming home.'

The guards blocked the corridor. Two, maybe three. I was not sure. In the Deep, shadows sometimes counted as people. One had the Council's insignia on his shoulder. The other looked like someone who had once killed by accident and never cared much about it.

'Prince Tonny, you are ordered to return to the waiting hall. Your presence is —'

'Unauthorised. Yes, I heard that all through my childhood.' I took a step forward while Lucy followed behind me.

'You have three seconds to comply,' one said.

'And you have three to realise that if my hand lifts, you will have nothing left to grab.'

I did not know where that came from. Maybe it was the way they looked at me, like something they should have dealt with earlier but did not. Maybe it was Lucy standing behind me, and the knowledge that she still carried part of my power and would have stepped forward first if needed. So I did. One of them reached out with a move so clean and professional it could have won an award in a film.

He touched me, or thought he did. And then it happened. He froze. His hand passed through me like mist, and he hesitated. His eyes twitched, wanting to say something, but he did not. I was a bit to the side. Though present, I was not where I needed to be.

'What... what was that?' the second one shouted. 'This is not possible!'

Moving just a step, I became aware of the delay. My foot landed before they saw it. My voice came a second ahead.

'Funny,' I said, smiling. 'What five days in another world can do to you, right?'

'Grab him!' one shouted.

But when they ran, they chased an echo. I was always a fraction of a moment out of reach, jumping over a shadow just as they stepped into it. One swung, and his sword cut through the air where I had been a second earlier, but not where I was now. Lucy stood back, eyes wide, wanting to say something. With a delay, she probably missed what I said.

'I… I do not know what I am doing,' I told her. But it reached her a second late.

Then I ran. The guards panicked, because there was nowhere to hit me. My voice came from the right. Footsteps sounded to the left. My body? Who knew.

One of them shouted, 'This is not allowed!'

I stopped. Smiled.

'I am not here for permission.'

Then I breathed on his face, no magic, just air. But he stepped back as if I had breathed truth into him. Grabbing Lucy's hand, I ran.

Chapter Thirty
The Moment

Through corridors, shadow after shadow, light chasing its own echo. Shouting, confusion, and an uncatchable silence were all I left behind.

There he was.

With his eyes, my father opened them. They were green. Bright, sharp, and completely awake. There was no confusion in them, but full awareness. Our gazes locked, the world paused, and then he whispered, 'Tonny?'

Everything I had carried for so long, all the pain, all the pressure in my chest, all the silence that had built up inside me, began to fall away. I was holding his hand.

'Dad, I missed you. Everything went upside down and I thought... well, that you were dead. And then Alan, and then I went—'

'Shhh. I know. I know everything,' Father said. His voice was quiet.

I helped him sit up after I moved closer. His skin looked pale, and his body felt weak. Lucy stood quietly behind me, saying nothing.

'I knew someone was trying to reach me. That's why I gave your power to Lucy, to protect it. I didn't realise it was my own father I needed to protect you from,' he said.

I blinked. The words stung.

'Protect me from him?'

Slowly the door opened, quiet as a breath. The room shifted around us. He had come.

Grandfather, Alfonzo De Death.

He stood tall. His coat was black and clean. Neat hair, a face without age, and eyes as blank as space itself. We stayed silent. I felt my body tense, ready for whatever was coming. Lucy gasped. Father gripped my arm. Alfonzo looked at us for a long moment. Then he stepped forward. His shoes made no noise on the floor.

'So. You have woken him,' he said. His voice wasn't cruel. It was... tired. Father tried to rise, but Alfonzo raised a hand. 'Don't. You are too weak.'

I felt anger rise in me. 'Stay away from him!'

Alfonzo's gaze moved to me. Seeing sorrow in those eyes for the first time was unexpected.

'You think I harmed him. You think I silenced him for power. But you are wrong.'

'Then why?' I asked. My voice shook despite myself.

'Because someone else was moving in the Deep. Someone who wanted to take what belongs to you, Tonny. What belongs to all of us. I could not risk your father falling into their hands. I put him to sleep to keep him safe. To keep you both safe.'

The room became silent. Even the walls seemed to listen.

'I let them believe I was the tyrant,' Alfonzo continued. 'It was easier. Better that they feared me than that they saw the true danger coming. I have been watching, searching, waiting for the one who stirs against us. And they are still out there.'

Father breathed heavily, his hand trembling against mine. 'I thought you betrayed me.'

Alfonzo's expression softened, just slightly. 'No, my son. I have never betrayed you. I guarded you, even when you hated me for it.'

With a dry throat, I looked at him. Part of me still wanted to resist, to push him away, but another part knew he was telling the truth. The weight in his voice wasn't the weight of a liar. It was the weight of someone who had carried a secret for too long.

Lucy spoke at last. 'So you... you're not here to fight?'

'Fight?' Alfonzo shook his head. 'No. The battle is not with me. It is with the one who still hides in the shadows of the Deep. The one who wanted your father gone. The one who thought you were too young, Tonny, too unprepared to stand in their way.'

'But Alan... he...' Tonny said.

'Alan didn't know better, and he will pay for his sins!' He looked at me fully then, and I felt the air change. 'I did not come to end you. I came to stand with you.'

At that moment, the doors burst open and hit the walls. The sound was sharp, shaking the whole palace. And then the Deepers arrived. They came all at once, not soldiers but a festival crowd, bursting in with noise and energy.

Each one looked different, and most of them looked more strange than dangerous. Some had feathers in their hair. One wore a lantern on his head. Another walked backwards and said it kept evil spirits away. Someone else had saucepans strapped to his back, making loud clanking noises as he walked. A tall figure came in carrying a huge wooden spoon instead of a weapon. Almost none of them wore armour.

At the front was Maria. Her apron was stained red, and she held a whisk like it was a weapon. Her face showed pride and determination. Martus was next to her. He held his needles like weapons too, but he looked more surprised than ready to fight.

'This… this is complete nonsense,' he muttered.

A Deeper wearing a flowerpot on his head spun around and shouted, 'Is this it? Where's the villain? Where's the traitor?'

Then they saw us. And they stopped. Lucy was safe. My father was sitting up. I was standing. And Alfonzo… was with us.

Maria blinked, lifting her arms and shouted, 'What?'

'We came to rescue!' said the one holding a hoe.

'I brought a cake!' someone added. The cake was upside down and a bit squashed.

I raised my hands. 'It's all right.'

The noise stopped. The room went quiet. One Deeper gently set a cauldron on the floor. Another took off his helmet. A third wiped his eyes and started crying.

'I was really looking forward to it,' he said. 'I had a speech. It rhymed.'

Looking at Martus, Maria sighed. 'Tell me we didn't run across the whole Deep for nothing.'

Martus opened his old guidebook and turned a page. 'Chapter twenty-nine. Heroic arrivals are rarely on time. Especially not in the Deep.'

No one laughed. Instead, the room grew quiet again. A Deeper looked up and froze. One by one, they all turned to face the same direction. Their eyes were on my father. In the centre of the room, he stayed silent and motionless. There was no hint of coldness or threat, just stillness.

Standing the way he did, he seemed strong. His appearance suggested that he had been through a lot and still decided to come back.

With her hands, Maria covered her mouth. Her eyes filled with tears. Martus lowered his head, his needles trembling. The Deepers began to kneel. Not all together. Some took their time. Others dropped quickly. No plan guided them, no order was given, but before long they were kneeling. And among them stood Alfonzo, no longer a shadow to fear, but the one who had guarded the flame in silence.

With Lucy on one side, my father on the other, and my grandfather beside us, I stood there. Feeling the Deep settle happened for the first time. It wasn't trembling. It wasn't broken. It was waiting. Then Alfonzo spoke, his voice low and steady.

'You wonder who it is. Who tried to take him from us. Who moves behind curtains while we tear ourselves apart. I have followed their shadow, but I do not yet know the face. Only this: they are close. Closer than you think.'

My chest tightened. The thought that it could be anyone, even someone I knew, pressed down on me. Lucy gripped my arm, because she seemed to feel the same.

'So who is it?' I asked.

Father looked at me, his green eyes sharp. He might answer, I thought for a moment. But instead he shook his head.

'That will be dealt with later. There is something else we must face first.'

The room became silent. Even the clatter of spoons and pots from the Deepers faded into nothing. He placed his hand on my shoulder. His touch was weak, but his gaze was strong.

'Tonny, it is time. The Deep needs more than my return. It needs a future. You are no longer just my son. You are an heir. And you must be crowned.'

The words hit me like a stone dropped into water, sending ripples through every part of me. I had wanted him back, I had wanted answers, I had even wanted peace. But this? To stand where he once stood? To carry everything? I opened my mouth, but nothing came out.

'Not today,' Father said, as though he could hear the storm inside me. 'But soon. The next chapter belongs to you.'

The Deepers lifted their heads. Their eyes were on me now, not on him. I felt Lucy's hand slip into mine. Feeling my grandfather's steady presence, I was comforted. I felt the weight of the Deep pressing in, not as an enemy, but as something waiting to be claimed.

I drew a slow breath. It no longer felt as if I were waiting for someone else to act. The Deep was waiting for me, and I knew this was only the beginning.

Maria gave Martus a sharp nudge.

'Have you noticed anything?' she whispered. He bobbed his head quickly, not really looking. 'Go on, look properly.'

With his eyes darting over her face, Martus leaned closer.

'Er... you've got a bit of dust in your hair?'

Maria puffed her lips in annoyance.

'Not that, you hopeless thing. My skin. It's still the same. You said it would change back.'

Blinking, Martus's mouth hung open.

'That's... impossible.'

'I don't know why,' she said softly, lowering her eyes. 'But I rather like it.'

'I liked you anyway... with or without the ladles.'

www.ingramcontent.com/pod-product-compliance
Lightning Source LLC
Chambersburg PA
CBHW060357260626
47160CB00006B/2347